MW01490183

to all
characters
I've killed
before

TROUBLE IN LOVE SERIES

BOOK 3

Jessie Cal

TO ALL CHARACTERS I'VE KILLED BEFORE

Contents

If you've ever wondered what a writer's mind is like... Trust me, you don't wanna know.

"Falling in love with you was the most liberating experience that has ever happened to me, and I will never kill that..."

Chapter 1

M OST PEOPLE WOULDN'T CHOOSE the roof of their five-story building as a place of meditation, but Victorine Leesky wasn't like most people.

As *a New York Times* best-selling author, she prided herself in being creative with all her thriller books. But this one, out of all the rest, needed to be her best one yet. She was being nominated for a Platinum Pen—the highest award for a thriller writer. All she needed to do was figure out how to kill Emily, her female character, and publish her book before the deadline.

She jumped up on the ledge and closed her eyes, feeling the icy wind brush against her short brown hair and fair skin. The sound of cars and motor-cycles rushing by on the street below helped her to visualize what it would be like if Emily got hit by a car.

No.

Too cliché.

She needed more tension.

She took a deep breath and focused on the different sounds from a construction site nearby. *Could something fall on her?*

"Let me guess..." A woman came from behind, chewing her gum so loudly, it threw Victorine off her train of thought. Not that it was going anywhere, anyway. "You're still not done with the book?"

Victorine opened her eyes and let out a frustrated sigh. Jumping down from the ledge, she spotted Tess pulling her long black hair in a high ponytail before caressing her pregnant belly.

"Why do you bother having a phone if it's never on you?" Tess grumbled, out of breath. "How do you even manage to be away from it?" It was obviously a rhetorical question. Tess worked in the marketing department at Blazing Hearts Publishing with Anne-Marie, Victorine's sister, and she was the type of woman who simply could not go one day without checking social media.

"I don't like being bothered when I'm meditating," Victorine said, only to get a moody glare from Tess.

"You know who else doesn't like being bothered? This guy!" She pointed to her belly. "I don't know why people say being pregnant is wonderful. Is that some sick prank from one mother to another? It's gotta be. And feeling the baby kick, by the way, is *not* amazing. You would think that after five kids, one gets used to it, but no. It's still weird, and it freaks me out."

"You have such a glow when you talk about your pregnancy," Victorine teased, leaning back against the ledge.

"You want a suggestion on how to kill your character?" Tess said, making a huge bubble out of her gum then popping it. "Get her to mess with a hormonal pregnant woman. Fatal result, guaranteed."

When Tess popped her gum again, Victorine cringed, then turned toward the crowded street to distract herself from her own idiosyncrasy.

"So, what's going on?" Tess came to stand next to Victorine. "Cutting this close to the deadline isn't like you."

When she popped the gum again, Victorine stuck out her hand in front of Tess's face. "Spit it out."

"You're kidding—"

"Now." Victorine wasn't rude. But she also wasn't going to argue.

As soon as Victorine had Tess's gum in her hand, she threw it over the edge with a second thought.

"I can't seem to figure out how to kill Emily," Victorine said as if she hadn't just thrown a huge piece of gum on passersby. "This has never happened to me before." Maybe the pressure of the writer's award was looming over her head and creating a mental block? It had to be.

"Why does she have to die at all?" Tess asked.

"Because it's a thriller."

"Then why not kill someone else?"

Victorine rolled her eyes. Clearly, she was talking to the wrong person about this. "She just has to die, okay."

"Fine. Either way, I just came to let you know that your sister will be out of the office for a week. She was assigned to a writing retreat."

"A writing retreat?" Victorine echoed. "When did she start writing?"

"She hasn't," Tess said. "She's there to meet with an author. Well, more like *persuade* him. Either way, it's not as good as it sounds. She'll fill you in later. Anyway, our boss says you may have to email the manuscript this time since Anne-Marie will be away and your manuscript is due in a week."

"I don't send my manuscripts through email, you know that." Victorine didn't even own a computer. She wrote all of her books on a typewriter and handed the only copy of her manuscript to Anne-Marie, who worked for her publisher. "And no one gets my first draft before my sister."

"There's gotta be a parking spot available!" A man's voice rang with irritation from across the roof and Tess turned around. "I'll take two blocks away if that's the best you can do."

"Who's that?" Tess asked.

Victorine didn't have to turn around to recognize her neighbor's voice. Charles was the only other person who ever came up to the roof as often as she did. "My neighbor. He doesn't get good reception in his apartment."

"How do you know that?"

"He only comes up here to talk on the phone."

"Maybe he doesn't want his wife to hear?"

"He lives by himself."

"Then maybe he's looking for an opportunity to talk to you." Tess bumped her hip on Victorine's side, and she snorted.

"Nonsense."

"How can you be so sure?"

Victorine looked at Tess. "Because he's a therapist, which means he can sense troubled minds from a mile away. So, no. I don't think he would hang around, hoping to strike a conversation with a woman who stands on a ledge as part of her research."

"Have you two ever talked?"

"One time." Victorine glanced at him. His dirty blond hair was buzzed down again, and his light sweater hugged his narrow waist just right.

"And what happened?" Tess pressed.

"Nothing." Victorine looked away from Charles and back to Tess. "He asked if I needed any help, and I just told him it was for a book I was writing. He never bothered me again."

"Bothered?" Tess's mouth dropped. "A hunk like that strikes up a conversation and it's a *bother* to you?"

"Oh, please." Victorine rolled her eyes. "He probably thought I was going to jump off and wanted to be a good Samaritan."

"Well, you seem to know a lot about this *good Samaritan*," Tess teased. "Just saying."

"I observe people so I can write about them," Victorine explained. "But that doesn't mean I know everything. He could still be a serial killer, keeping his victims in a storage unit..." Victorine's eyes widened with sudden clarity, then her mouth dropped open. "Oh my goodness, that's it!"

"What?"

"Of course..."

"What?" Tess asked again. "Earth to Victorine!"

Victorine looked at Tess with an excited grin. "I know why I haven't been able to kill Emily!"

"Why?"

"Because it's not about Emily at all." She chuckled as if it should've been obvious. "It's about the killer! I gotta go."

"Where?"

Victorine was already headed toward the staircase. "Tell Anne-Marie the book will be ready this week!"

Chapter 2

AT THE CHILDREN'S CARE facility, Victorine spotted six-year-old Ari jumping on her bed by the window, watching the latest football highlights on TV. Ari was Michelle's sister. As for Michelle, she was Victorine's foster sister along with Faye, Anne-Marie, and Judy. The five of them had lived in the same foster home for years, and had been part of each other's lives ever since.

"Aunt Vicky!" Ari cheered as Victorine finally walked in, holding a teddy bear hugging a stuffed football. "Is that for me?"

"That depends. Have you been behaving?" Victorine asked, and Ari shook her head with a mischievous grin. "That's my girl." She handed Ari the stuffed animal and watched as her face lit up.

"Thank you, Aunt Vicky." Ari gave Victorine a tight hug.

"You're welcome, gremlin." Victorine kissed the top of her head then sat next to her on the bed. "So, what should we name him?"

"It's not a *he*..." Ari corrected, opening the bear's legs. "See, there's nothing there."

Victorine's eyes widened in surprise. "Does Michelle know about your newfound knowledge?"

Ari giggled, and Victorine's eyes darted toward the nurse who had walked in a minute ago.

"She found a male baby doll in the donated pile of toys," the nurse explained. "It peed, so your sister had to explain what it was."

Ari giggled again, and Victorine chuckled. She would've paid to have seen Michelle get through that conversation. Michelle was the most conservative out of all of the girls. Even though Victorine hadn't been on a date in months, her books had more than their share of spice.

"Can I ask you a question?" Victorine asked the nurse as she flushed Ari's IV. "Hypothetically speaking... as a nurse, have you ever thought about killing someone?"

The nurse's eyes widened in horror.

"It's for a book," Ari explained with another giggle. "My auntie is an author. Isn't that right, Aunt Vicky?"

The nurse grumbled something under her breath as she finished with the IV and headed toward the door.

"Maybe *I* can help?" Ari looked up at Victorine with an eager spark in her brown eyes. "Are you still writing about Daniel?"

It warmed her heart how Ari remembered her character's names without even a second thought. "No, Daniel is fine. Emily is the one in a little bit of trouble right now. I just need to figure out where to go from there."

"He saves her and she marries him," Ari says like it should've been obvious, and Victorine chuckled.

"All right, Miss Happy-Ending... What book am I reading to you today?" Victorine leaned back on the bed as Ari reached for a book on the nightstand. *The Prince and His Bride*, again. Victorine lost count of how many times she read that one, but she couldn't bear to disappoint those big brown eyes.

"You know these cheesy love stories make me gag, right?"

Ari giggled. "That's what makes it funny."

"Ah, I'm glad that amuses you." Next time, instead of a teddy bear, maybe Victorine should bring her a new book. As she opened the cover, Ari snuggled into her arms.

"Do any of your characters have a rare blood disease like me?" Ari asked, her tone already tired from the meds the nurse had dosed her with.

"No, they don't."

She looked up and met Victorine's eyes. "Why not?"

"Because I don't write about superheroes. And you, little missy..." She poked Ari's nose. "Are a superhero. You got that?"

Ari nodded then shifted her gaze back to the book. "Can you make the Prince have that funny accent, again?"

"Sure." When Ari snuggled further into her arms, Victorine knew she would read that book for the rest of her life if Ari wanted her to. "Anything you want."

Later that night, after spending hours staring at her typewriter, unable to think of a good enough sentence to start the new chapter, Victorine decided she needed some inspiration. Grabbing a notebook and pen, she sat on the sofa and pressed play to continue watching where she left off of her favorite criminal show.

Fifteen minutes into the episode, she had already handwritten two pages of ideas in her notebook. Her mental juices were finally flowing, the only problem was... Emily kept trying to survive. She was quite the fighter. People never gave blondes much credit, but Emily was as strong as she was smart. She would not go down without a fight, and the more Victorine wrote, the more Emily resisted.

Victorine paused her notes and stared at the scribbled paper as if staring at a picture of Emily. She smiled, feeling a sense of pride toward Emily with her strong nature. Though Emily was certain to die, Victorine couldn't write her off like she had done previous characters. Emily deserved better.

Victorine shifted her attention back to the show for the reveal of the killer. Her pen hovering eagerly over the page, feeling the buildup of inspiration slowly bubbling up inside. But then the lights went out and the TV turned off, leaving Victorine sitting in the dark with the same mental block as before.

Oh. No, no, no.

She jumped to her feet and went to the pantry in search of a flashlight. She hadn't been able to write a decent sentence for days, and now that she finally got going, she would not allow anything to suck her back into the mental rut she'd been struggling with.

No way.

Grabbing the flashlight, she clicked it on and went to check on her fuse box. She flipped a few of the switches but it made no difference. Only the light from the busy street reflected on her ceiling.

She let out a long sigh, hating how often the power was cut off in her building. Normally she didn't mind because she would have a candle burning and her typewriter ferociously working. But it wasn't one of those nights, and her only source of inspiration was the TV, which meant she needed it back on sooner rather than later.

She slipped into her coat and headed up to the roof. As soon as she stepped outside, the icy cold wind hit her in the face and she wrapped her coat tighter around her thin body. She looked around, pointing the flashlight as she searched for the metal box. She'd seen the electrician here last week messing with it.

There it is!

She rushed to the box and wasn't surprised to find the lock missing. There were so many problems in that old building, certainly a missing lock hadn't become a priority.

She held the flashlight between her teeth and opened the door to have a better look.

"What are you doing?" a deep voice called out from behind her, and she turned around, flashing the blinding light in Charles' eyes.

"Oh, sorry." She grabbed the flashlight and pointed back into the metal box. "I'm just trying to get the power working."

"The power is out again?" he asked, shoving his cell into his back pocket. "Wait, I thought you were a writer, not an electrician."

"How do you know what I do for a living?" she asked without bothering to look back. The sooner she got the power going, the sooner she could go back to finishing her book.

"My secretary is obsessed with your books," he said, coming to look over her shoulder. "Now, please tell me you know what you're doing."

"I'll have you know…" She scanned through the labels until she found a red switch. "My last character was an electrician, so… I've done a lot of research."

"You're kidding, right?"

She hooked her finger on the switch then looked at him. "I never kid about research." She flipped it on and a bright spark shot off like a firework, sending a current of electricity up her arm. Her back hit the concrete floor, as did her head. She grimaced as the throbbing pain spread around her skull. She closed her eyes as the tingly sensation traveled up her arms and down her spine.

Ouch.

By the time she opened her eyes, Charles' deep blues were hovering over her. "Are you okay?" he asked, holding her head. "Victorine?"

"I'm good." She winced as she tried to sit up.

"Easy now." He pulled her up gently then held her steady as her head began to spin. "Do you need me to call an ambulance?"

"No, I'm okay," she assured him.

"How many fingers am I holding up?" he asked anyway, and she shoved his hand away.

"I'm fine, really." She touched the back of her head. It wasn't throbbing as much anymore, but she would definitely be fighting a headache later on. "Hey! It worked!" She pointed to the light near the door. It was faint, but it was on, nonetheless. Now, she could finish her episode and continue with her book.

She turned to Charles with a pleased smile, and he let out a disbelieving chuckle. "You're a strange girl," he said, shaking his head. "Come on, I'll walk back with you."

He helped her to her feet, and she held onto his arm, which was surprisingly firm. He didn't strike her as the type who worked out often, but those biceps didn't appear by chance.

"Thanks," she said, pulling back and smoothing her shirt. "You don't have to go out of your way for me. I'm fine."

"That's all right." He reached for the door and held it open for her. "I was on my way back, anyway."

They went down the stairs then walked in silence until they finally reached her door. "Well, this is me," she said, pointing to the number nine just above her peephole. "Thanks for walking me back... even though you're right next door."

"Thank *you* for saving me from a cold shower." Victorine cocked her head as if he had said something inappropriate, and he chuckled.

"I'm referring to the power coming back on."

"Oh, right!" Her cheeks flushed and she turned away to open the door. "Good night, Charles."

He offered a polite nod as he turned to walk away. "Good night, Victorine."

After taking a shower and popping an ibuprofen, Victorine was able to finish the episode but couldn't bring herself to write anything new. So she turned off the TV and got tucked into bed. Closing her eyes, she began to visualize the last scene she'd written. *Emily had been taken from the hospital by a nurse who... was the killer? No... related to the killer?*

"What if there is no killer?"

Victorine chuckled as if the thought itself was absurd. "How could a thriller not have a killer? Nonsense."

"Then kill someone else."

Victorine opened her eyes, realizing the voice wasn't inside her head. She turned to look and saw a young man with dark, messy hair lying on the bed next to her.

Victorine screamed as she rolled off the mattress and onto the carpet. "Stay back!" she yelled, looking for something to defend herself with. All she could find was a hardcover book on her nightstand. She grabbed it and aimed it at the young man, who was now on his feet looking quite amused.

"What... you're going to *papercut* me to death?" he teased, but Victorine didn't think it was funny. Not one bit.

"Who are you?" she asked, keeping the book in front of her as if it were a real weapon. "And how did you get into my apartment?"

"You don't recognize me?" the young man asked, crossing his arms and leaning against the dresser. "That hurts. I thought I meant more to you."

She lowered the book and took a few seconds to *really* look at him. He wore a leather jacket and jeans, and though she was never opposed to the bad boy vibe, she had never dated someone younger than her. "Look, clearly you're mistaking me for someone else—"

"There is no mistaking Victorine Leesky." He flashed her a smile so sexy it would definitely melt a crowd of high school girls. But not her. She had been done with high school for over ten years now.

"What do you want from me?" She raised the book again. "Is it money? I might have a few hundred dollars in my purse, but that's about it."

"I don't want your money," he said, turning serious. "I want to know how to get Emily back."

Victorine gave him a puzzled look. "Excuse me?"

"Emily..." he repeated. "She was taken, and I need to get her back before you kill her."

Victorine's mouth dropped, as did her hands. "Is this a joke?"

"Does it look like a joke? Actually..." He raised a hand. "Don't answer that. The point is... I'm here to stop you from killing Emily."

Victorine rushed to the living room. Her manuscript was exactly where she had left it—next to her typewriter by the window. That was the only copy of her book that existed. How in the world did he know about Emily?

She turned around and found him leaning against the doorway. "Who are you?" she asked again, moving away from him. "And how in the world do you know about Emily?"

"You know who I am."

She shook her head as she reached for the loose manuscript on the desk. She shoved it into a large envelope then pressed it to her chest. "How dare you come into my house and look through my unfinished manuscript."

"I didn't look through your book."

"Then how do you know what's in it?"

"You know who I am."

"Stop that."

"Just say it."

"Get out of my house."

"Tell me where Emily is."

"I'm calling the police." She reached for the phone, all the while watching him plop down on the sofa in front of her.

"What are you gonna tell them, huh? A character from your book is harassing you? I hardly doubt that will work in your favor."

The police operator came on the other line and Victorine opened her mouth, but she couldn't respond. *Could this really be happening?* "No... absolutely not. You are *not* Daniel!"

"What's your emergency?" the woman on the other line asked for the second time, and Daniel grabbed the phone.

"Please send someone over! This woman is threatening to kill my girlfriend!"

"Stop it!" Victorine snatched the phone from his hand. "That is not true! Don't listen to him!"

There was silence on the other end but only for a moment. "I'm sorry, what's your emergency, ma'am?"

Victorine's eyes widened, and Daniel flashed a smug smile. "You didn't hear any of that?" Victorine asked, her voice barely audible.

"Hear what, ma'am? Are you in danger?"

"Uh, no. It's nothing, sorry..." Victorine hung up the phone and stared at Daniel, who was now lying on the sofa with a smug look on his face.

"Told ya."

"I must be asleep." She threw the manuscript back on the table then headed to the kitchen. After turning on the faucet, she splashed a handful of water on her face then dried it with a paper towel. "And this is just a bad dream."

When she opened her eyes, Daniel was standing so close, she jumped back with a shriek. "Get away from me!"

"Can we talk like adults?"

"No... you are not real." Victorine threw her coat over her pajamas then grabbed her purse and rushed out the door, leaving him in the apartment. She ran down the hall and hurried into the opened elevator, pressing the button over and over again for the door to close before he came after her.

When the door finally shut and the elevator started its descent, she leaned back against the wall and closed her eyes. *What was happening to her?*

"Why do you keep fighting this?" Victorine shot her eyes open only to find Daniel standing across from her, leaning back with his arms crossed. "The sooner we talk about why I'm here, the sooner I'll leave you alone."

She turned toward the closed door and watched as the floor numbers counted down.

"Ignoring me won't work," he said, but she ignored him anyway. When the elevator pinged, she darted across the lobby and toward the exit. The icy chill hit her face as soon as she stepped outside. "Where could you possibly be going at this ungodly hour?"

"To get rid of you." She turned to face him with a glare so intense, a couple walking by moved away from her. She smiled at them sheepishly. Once they continued on their way, she turned to Daniel again. "And I know just the place."

Chapter 3

THE NEXT MORNING, VICTORINE woke up at the ER. The sound of a curtain being pushed aside hit her ears at full volume, and she turned to see a doctor approaching her gurney.

"How are you feeling?" he asked, looking up from her chart.

"That depends..." she said, groggy from sleep. "Did my results come back?"

"They did, and everything looks good. No concussion," he said, flipping through the pages he was holding. "It might've just been exhaustion. That's why we gave you some sleeping pills last night."

She hadn't had a good night's sleep ever since she hit a mental block in her writing, but what did that have to do with what was happening to her?

"That can't be right." Victorine snatched the folder from his hands. "What about the CT scan?" She skimmed through the pages, but her eyes could barely focus. "There's gotta be something wrong, I mean... I got electrocuted and hit my head pretty hard on the concrete."

"And miraculously, you seem perfectly fine. Like I said... it could've just been exhaustion. The brain needs its rest."

"What about the MRI?" she pressed. "Are you sure I don't have a concussion?"

"I checked everything, Ms. Leesky," he assured her. "There's nothing wrong with you."

She scanned her small room, and to her relief, Daniel was gone. Could sleep have been all she needed to get rid of him?

"I will print out a list of therapists for you," the doctor said, and Victorine looked at him in confusion. "You know... in case you want to talk to someone."

"About what?" Had he heard her talking to Daniel last night? Much of the night before was hazy in her mind, but it didn't matter. Daniel was finally gone and that was all she cared about. "Never mind."

"I'll include the list with your discharge papers."

"Fine." Victorine handed him back her chart. She was too tired to argue. "Where is the restroom?"

"Down the hall to the left."

"Thank you."

Once he walked away, she grabbed her purse and started down the hall. The restroom wasn't as close as she thought it would be. Either that or she had gotten lost. That hospital was like a maze. She finally found a family room somewhere in a deserted wing and went inside. She hurried to the faucet and splashed cold water on her face, feeling relieved that Daniel was finally gone. After drying her face with a paper towel, she walked out of the restroom, only to realize she had already forgotten how to get back to her bed. Her brain was still in a fog, and it didn't help that there were no signs to guide her back.

She did find a sign that caught her eye, though, and she had to do a double take. *The morgue*. She had never seen one before. Did they have freezers like in the movies? It would be good research for a scene.

Her plan was simply to have a peek through the window, but when she spotted a nurse walking out, she couldn't pass up the opportunity. Before her brain could warn her against it, she hurried into the room, letting the door close behind her. The room was a lot colder than the rest of the hospital, and the lights were dim as she walked toward a metal table in the back.

"This is creepy." A voice came from behind her, and she spun around.

"You again!"

"Can we argue somewhere else?" Daniel replied, glancing over his shoulder at the three white sheets in the center of the room. "This place is giving me the creeps."

She let out an exasperated breath. "So much for everything being *perfectly fine*."

"If you touch a dead body, I swear I will barf."

"Of course I won't," she snapped, reaching for a folder on the table and flipping through the pages. "I'm just curious to know how they died."

"Well, hurry up." Daniel moved closer to her as if the bodies under the sheets could attack him at any moment.

"I shouldn't have written you to be such a wimp."

"Isn't that the truth," he muttered, peeking at the files she was reading. "What are you looking for, anyway?" When Victorine didn't respond,

Daniel grunted. "Why are you so insistent on killing her?"

"Because it's a thriller, Daniel. I'm sorry."

He grabbed the folder from her and threw it back on top of the table, forcing her to look at him. "Then kill someone else."

"That's not how it works."

"Sure it is."

Victorine crossed her arms and leaned against the metal table. "Then please, enlighten me."

"Kill the *killer*!"

Victorine didn't even know who the killer was yet, but it didn't matter because no one knew more about her books than her. "Why am I even having this conversation with you? You're not real." As she reached for the folder again, Daniel stepped in front of her. "Okay, fine. What's it gonna take for you to leave me alone?"

"Tell me how to save Emily."

"She can't be saved."

"Why not?"

"Because..." A million reasons ran through her mind, but only one was clear enough in that moment. "I want the Platinum Pen."

"What the heck is a Platinum Pen?"

"Every thriller writer's dream award. But I don't expect you to understand."

Daniel stared at her as if she'd slapped him. "You're killing the love of my life so you can win an *award*?"

Voices came from the hallway, and Victorine hurried to look through the rectangle glass on the door. "Great, you wasted all my time." When she turned around, Daniel was gone. She shook off the feeling of guilt that tugged at her heart and reminded herself that she wasn't doing anything wrong. He wasn't real, and neither was his life with Emily.

The door opened, and she straightened her posture like a little kid caught red-handed. "Oh, hi. I was looking for the restroom?"

The nurse gave Victorine a skeptical look then opened the door wider. "It's across the hall."

"Thank you." Victorine hurried past the nurse and down the hall. By the time she finally returned to the ER, her discharge papers were ready.

"So, where do I sign?" she asked, and the nurse at the front desk pointed to the bottom of the page. Victorine scribbled her signature then handed the paper back with the pen.

"Oh, and here's a list of therapists the doctor recommends."

"I don't need a shrink." Victorine raised a hand. "I just need to finish my book."

·♥·♥·♥·♥·♥·

Victorine cringed in front of her typewriter with every chew of Daniel's gum as he sat across from her with his feet popped up on her desk. He was purposely trying to distract her so she couldn't focus on her writing, but he was not going to win.

She stood and walked toward her stereo and popped in a Hans Zimmer CD. She cranked it up at full volume before sitting back down. When she realized she could no longer hear him chewing, she flashed him a smug smile then resumed typing. Even though every sentence was going to be utter garbage, she needed to keep writing because something was always better than nothing. As Anne-Marie always said: *you can't edit a blank page.*

If Victorine could just finish the book, then maybe Daniel would disappear from her mind once and for all.

After a few minutes typing fiercely on her typewriter, she was startled by a loud knock on her door. She huffed with annoyance when Daniel flashed a pleased smile. "Enjoy your smugness while it lasts," she warned. "I'm finishing this book and getting rid of you."

Another loud knock came from the door, and she hurried to lower the volume on the stereo before walking to the door and looking through the peephole.

Charles!

She yanked the door open. "Just the person I needed to see!" Before he even had a chance to speak, she grabbed him by the arm and pulled him inside. She kicked the door closed then noticed Daniel was gone. *Good.* She turned to face Charles, who had his brows arched as he watched her. "I need to ask you a question."

"Okay..."

"So, I've been having trouble figuring out a way to kill one of my characters. But now there's this really *annoying voice* in my head that is very distracting and doesn't let me focus."

"So, what's your question?"

"How do I get rid of it?"

Charles shrugged. "What makes you think I would know?"

She looked at him with a perplexed look. "Don't therapists like...analyze their patients and help them to understand their thoughts or whatnot?"

Charles smiled. "First of all..." He raised a finger. "It takes more than one session to get to that point. And second..." He raised another finger. "You're not my patient."

"Oh, I'm not asking you to be my therapist," she clarified. "I'm just asking your opinion... you know, as a friend."

Charles flashed her another amused smile. "Good night, Victorine."

"Charles, please..." She jumped in front of him, blocking the door. "I am begging you. If I don't get this voice out of my head, I won't be able to finish this book, and if it's not published by next month, I won't get the Platinum Pen."

He watched her for a long moment, then let out a defeated breath. "What exactly is it that you need?"

"How do I get rid of him?"

"Him?"

Crap. "Well, I mean... every nagging voice I've ever heard has come from a man so... it's more than fitting."

Charles chuckled. "So, what does *he* want from you?"

"He wants me to change the story and give them a happy ending."

"But you don't want to do that?"

"I can't," Victorine explained. "I always kill the female characters in my books. It's my *thing*. It's been my thing since my very first release. If I make an exception for Emily, it will throw my readers for a loop, and I can't afford to get bad reviews on this book because I'm being nominated for an award. Now, of course, I made the mistake of telling him about that," she mumbled quickly. "Now, he's being even more obnoxious than before."

Charles gave her a curious look. "And this voic e... is it from one of your characters?"

Victorine stared at him, wishing she had been more vague. "Now, that's an interesting theory." She played it off. "What else you got? Hypothetically speaking, that is."

He chuckled, and noticing his dimples for the first time made her cheeks feel warm. She quickly shook it off and forced herself to focus on what he was saying. "It could be that this hypothetical character is coming from your subconscious."

"How so?"

"How do you feel about killing this... Emily character?" he asked, and Victorine thought about it for a moment.

"I'm not sure."

"Then maybe that's the question that needs to be answered," he said. "And until that happens, you may not be able to kill her."

"What if I can't answer that?" Victorine asked. "I mean, what if it's too complicated."

"Try writing her a letter," he suggested. "Maybe letting her know how you feel could help you move on."

"You want me to write a letter to a fictional character?"

"Treating her like a real person may help you to view your own feelings as real."

"Interesting."

"I hope it works out." He flashed her a heart-stopping smile before reaching for the door. "I should go. Thanks for turning the music down."

"Right. Sorry about that."

He pulled open the door then glanced over his shoulder. "Good night, Victorine."

She leaned against the doorway as he walked out. "Good night, Charles."

Chapter 4

T HE NEXT MORNING, VICTORINE poured a cup of coffee then went to catch the sunrise on the roof. It wasn't often that she did that. After all, she couldn't really see the sunrise from that spot except for the orange rays breaking through the highrises. But lately she felt a strong need for a little quiet, and that was the quietest time of the day in the city. The loud buzzing—at least on her street—didn't start until after seven, so she had about an hour of peace and relative quiet to think.

The air was cold, and she pulled her hoodie over her head. The coffee mug felt nice and warm on her fingers.

"You're up early," Charles said, coming to stand next to her with his own cup of coffee. "Couldn't sleep?"

"Sleep is overrated." She sipped her coffee and enjoyed the warmth that washed over her. "How about you?"

"Trying to figure out whether or not to pack my bags and leave for the weekend," he replied.

"Why the sudden escape?"

"My father's coming to the city for work, and I really don't want to be here when he shows up."

"Why not?"

"Because..." He let out a frustrated sigh. "He's gonna bug me about taking this job in England, and I really don't want to keep arguing about it."

"Then don't," she said, turning to face him. "What's keeping you from leaving?"

He shrugged. "I can't think of anywhere to go, I guess."

"Is that the only reason?"

"*That*, and..." He shifted his weight from one foot to the other. "I don't have anyone to go with. My sister is out of town with her boyfriend and... I can't really think of anyone else who would be up for a last-minute trip."

"I would be up for it," she said, gulping what was left of her drink. "And if you need a place to go, we could meet up with *my* sister."

"Is that a joke?"

"Not at all. You need a destination, and I need to get this manuscript off my hands sooner rather than later, so... I'll go with you."

"Are you even done with your book?" he asked.

"No, but..." She raised a hopeful finger. "I'm pretty sure if I left the city to a quieter place, I could finish it."

Charles leaned on the concrete ledge and narrowed his eyes. "You're serious about this?"

"Oh, I never kid about finishing a book," she said. "But you'll get to dodge your father's visit so... it's a win-win."

Charles thought about it for a few seconds. "Where's your sister staying?"

"South Carolina."

Charles laughed. "It's amazing how you make an eight-hour drive sound like it's just around the corner."

"I'll tell you what..." She put her cup down on the ledge and turned to face him. "You take me to see my sister, and I'll let you have my parking spot."

He narrowed his eyes at her again. "How do you know I've been trying to get a parking spot?"

"Well, it's not like you whisper when you're on the phone up here. Quite distracting, actually."

"Is that right?" He crossed his arms. "And which parking spot is yours, exactly?"

She hesitated but only for a moment. "The one by the back door."

"Are you kidding me?" He looked at her as if she'd slapped him. "I've been trying to get that spot for three years."

She flashed him an sheepish smile. "I know."

"You don't even own a car."

"It's for my sisters when they come to visit. They hate parking five blocks away."

"*I* have to park five blocks away. *Every. Day.*"

"Not anymore," she cheered, flashing him a cheesy smile. "So, what do you say, neighbor? Should we start packing?"

Hours later, Victorine waited in Charles' Subaru Forester as he went into a roadside diner to use the restroom. They had been on the road for hours, and she wasn't entirely sure if it was the trees or the single-lane roads that were filling her with inspiration, but she had already written six pages in her notebook.

If she had known that leaving the city was all she needed to get rid of her mental block, she would have done it weeks ago. And Daniel hadn't shown up to bother her, not once. She hadn't felt this relieved in weeks. Oh, how she missed feeling like herself again.

Though Emily was still alive, Victorine had a feeling she wasn't going to be for long. If she could only find a creek nearby, perhaps with a cottage, it would be perfect for her next scene. But what would be the procedure of finding a body near the water?

Surprisingly, none of her characters were ever found in a creek. Most of her thrillers took place in cities instead of small towns. Would the procedure be the same? When Victorine looked up from her notebook, she spotted a police officer walking out of the diner.

Perfect!

She rolled down the window and waited until the officer approached his vehicle, which was parked next to her. "May I ask you a quick question, Officer?"

He turned around. "How can I help you, ma'am?"

"Is there a creek around here?" she asked.

"There's Long Teeth Creek just about a few miles down that road," the officer replied, pointing in the direction of the creek.

"Great. Now, what would you do if you found a dead body near that creek?"

The officer's eyes shot open in alarm. "Excuse me?"

"What would be the procedure for finding a dead body near a creek?" She held up her notebook and started going down the list of possibilities she had written down. "Would you immediately call the homicide detectives, or would you do a perimeter check first? Wait, I guess that would depend on how long she's been dead, right?"

"I'm gonna need you to step out of the car, ma'am."

Victorine looked at the officer and noticed he had stepped away from her window for some reason. *Okay.* She put her notebook aside and stepped out of the car.

"Turn around and put your hands on the vehicle, please?"

"What?" It suddenly dawned on Victorine what was happening, and she laughed. "Oh! Okay, I see how bad this looks—"

"Hands on the vehicle."

"Officer, I was just doing research. Here, I'll show you my notebook." When she tried opening the door again, the officer grabbed her hand and twisted behind her back. She grimaced as he pressed her against the side of the car.

She tried explaining, but the officer was too busy stating her rights while handcuffing her. When he turned her around, she spotted Charles staring at her with his mouth agape.

"Oh, hey! Would you mind telling him that I was just—" The officer shoved her into the backseat of his cruiser and shut the door.

"Would you mind opening your trunk, sir?" the officer asked, walking toward the back of the car.

Charles let out a tired sigh as he placed the coffee cup on the hood of his car then reached for the key fob. "Let me guess..." he said, opening the trunk for the officer. "She asked you about police procedures in murder cases or whatnot?"

"I'm gonna need you to open these bags," the officer said, watching as Charles did what he asked. "Does she do this often?"

"I'm afraid so," Charles replied, stepping back after unzipping all of the bags. "That's Victorine Leesky. The thriller author from New York."

The officer looked at Charles in surprise. "You mean the writer of *Chasing Skulls*?"

That was the movie adaptation of one of her books, which Charles had never seen but spent hours that morning listening to Victorine talk about how it didn't do justice to her book. "That's the one."

"Why didn't she just say that?" The officer opened the door and helped her out. "My wife is obsessed with your books," he said, removing the handcuffs from her wrists. "Would you mind if I took a picture with you?"

"I don't really do pictures—"

"Sure, she would." Charles pinched her side, and she forced a smile. "After all, you're being such a nice guy for letting her go."

The officer handed Charles his smartphone then flashed a smile as he posed next to Victorine. "Can I also have your autograph?" he spoke through his wide grin. "I'm gonna give it to my wife along with your new book that's coming out in a few months. Oh, she's gonna freak out!"

After Charles snapped a few pictures, he handed the phone back to the giddy officer who already had a pen and his ticket notepad ready for Victorine to autograph. She scribbled on it and handed it back to him. "Thank you so much. Y'all have a good rest of your trip and be safe."

"Thank you, Officer." Charles waved until the officer drove off. "Well, that took an unexpected turn."

"I know," Victorine mumbled, crossing her arms. "He didn't answer any of my questions."

Charles gave her an amused smile. "Not quite what I was thinking but okay." He pulled the door open, and she got back in the passenger seat. He shut her door, and after grabbing the coffee from the hood, he jumped back in the driver's seat. But before he could turn on the engine, his phone rang.

He looked confused when he answered the call, and Victorine wondered who it was. "Hello? Yeah, this is he... Is she okay?... Are you sure?... Okay, I'll tell you what..." Charles glanced at his watch. "I'm just three hours away. I'll be right there. Thank you for the call."

After he hung up, Victorine turned to look at him. "Is everything okay?"

He let out a long sigh. "My grandmother's in the hospital."

"Is she okay?"

"She seems to be fine, but... I should still go check. It shouldn't take us too out of the way, though," he said, turning the key in the ignition. "She's in Virginia. Would it be okay if we swung by?"

"Of course." She opened her notebook and wrote the initials VA in the corner of her page with a question mark. "She wouldn't happen to live by a creek, now would she?"

Chapter 5

VICTORINE MOANED AS SHE took a bite out the most delicious pulled pork sandwich she'd ever had.

"Told you," Charles said with a satisfied smile. "This place has the best barbeque."

"Oh, this sauce!" she reveled with her mouth full. "It's amazing!"

"They make it fresh every day," he said. "In fact, this place was in one of those shows from *The Food Channel*. My grandfather loved it here."

Victorine moaned again. "It's heavenly."

Charles' phone rang, but when he silenced his ringer and continued with his dinner, she wiped her mouth.

"Was that your father again?" she asked, noticing he had ignored several of his calls during the drive.

"I already know what he wants," Charles admitted. "There's no need for him to keep calling, or even make a special trip to the city. I'm not changing my mind."

"About the job in England?"

"Not just that. He wants me back in the medical field."

"Aren't therapists already in the medical field?"

"Not according to Mr. Thoracic Surgeon." Charles deepened his voice to portray his father's authoritative tone. *"Therapy is nothing but soft science, son. You need to choose a real career."*

"Yikes."

"Oh, and that was him being nice." Charles chuckled, reaching for more fries. "Enough about me. Tell me about you. How did you get into writing?"

Victorine didn't have to think too hard. She remembered the exact day she started writing her first book. She was sixteen years old, and it was the first night in yet another foster home. It was also the first night away from her sisters after spending two years together in the same house. Victorine never seemed to mind the constant change. She was perfectly comfortable keeping to herself. But after bonding with those girls for two years, being separated from them was the hardest thing she ever had to do. She missed them terribly. Even though they kept in touch, it wasn't the same. Especially during storms, because that was when they would all huddle together on Victorine's bed and listen to her tell them stories all night. Not horror stories, though. Judy always liked fairy tales, and because she was the youngest, Victorine would give in. "I guess, the short answer is..." she said, "I wanted to escape reality."

"And the long answer?"

"Oh, I don't want to bore you."

Charles leaned forward on the table, his lips lifting at the corner. "Victorine Leesky may be a lot of things..." he said, holding her gaze. "But *boring* isn't one of them." He flashed her another heart-melting smile, and her cheeks turned hot. And when she couldn't look away, she found herself wondering *what type of aphrodisiac was in that barbeque sauce*?

"Are you ready to go?" he asked, taking one last sip from his water before pushing his chair back.

"What about the check?" she asked, looking around for their waitress.

"It's already taken care of," he said, waving it off. "I'm going to use the restroom before we go. There's still an hour left."

"Any update on your grandmother?"

"Yeah, they're waiting on the results of the X-ray. Looks like she might've broken her wrist."

"I'm sorry."

"That's all right." He rubbed his tired eyes. "I just want to get there and find out more details."

"Would you like me to drive the rest of the way?" she offered, and he gave her a skeptical look.

"Do you even know how to drive?"

She crossed her arms and narrowed her eyes. "Yes, Charles. I've driven a car before."

"All right." He pulled his keys from his pocket and handed it to her. "Just making sure."

When he finally dropped the keys in her hand, she beamed. "I got this."

"Watch out!"

Victorine veered away from the truck that sped past her, slamming on the horn. "Well, that was rude."

Charles was sweating with nerves. "*Rude* is not turning on your signal when switching lanes," he ground out through his tight jaw.

"I figure if I do it slowly enough, they would see me coming."

He let out a long breath, forcing himself to relax. "You said you knew how to drive."

"I said *I had driven before*," she corrected. "You don't want to know what happened to that car, though."

"Oh, great."

"It's fine. Look..." She pointed to the road. "As long as I stay in the slow lane, we're good."

"You've been behind this truck for forty-five minutes."

"Which means you could have taken a forty-five-minute nap by now but no...you keep bugging me. Besides, I only offered to drive to give you a break," she admitted. "You looked so tired. I couldn't have you sleep behind the wheel."

"Right... because your driving is so much safer for us—Victorine!"

Another truck sped by and she veered back into the slow lane, clutching the wheel for dear life. "See! That's exactly why I don't like switching lanes."

Charles let out another breath. "Forty more minutes," he whispered as if it were a silent prayer. "We can survive."

"So dramatic," she teased. "Why don't you put on some music? Distract yourself. I got this." She leaned forward and squinted at the road. When she bit her bottom lip in concentration, Charles found himself suppressing a smile.

"Fine." He grabbed his cell phone and started to scan through numerous playlists. "What kind of music do you like?"

"Pick whatever you want," she replied, still highly focused on the road even though she was only going fifty miles an hour behind a slow-moving truck.

"How about I shuffle through songs we both like? Give me an artist."

"Hans Zimmer."

Charles looked at her, surprised. "The movie soundtrack composer?"

"Yep. I don't care much for lyrics. It's not helpful when I'm writing. Although, I do like Enya."

"All right. Let's try it." He pressed play then slid his phone into the cup holder. "So, how's your book going?"

"Surprisingly well," she admitted. "I haven't been able to kill Emily yet but... it's getting close. I can feel it."

"Have you been able to pinpoint the real problem?"

"I think she's too much of a fighter," Victorine said as if it were a bad thing. "It doesn't matter how many dead-ends I put in her way, she always finds a way to survive."

"Sounds like a strong character."

"Oh, she's amazing."

"Could that be the problem?"

"What, exactly?"

"You like her."

"Of course I like her. I like all of my characters, but it has never made a difference before. They still die in the end. The million-dollar-question is... why can't I kill *her*?"

"Maybe not," Charles said, and Victorine glanced at him.

"What do you mean?"

"Maybe the *real* question isn't *why you can't kill her*," he suggested. "Maybe it's... *why won't you let her live?*"

"Well, I told you—"

"The writer's award, yes. But what's the *deeper* reason?" he asked. "Why did you start killing your characters to begin with? Perhaps understanding *that* can help you figure out what changed."

Victorine had never thought about it like that. It was an interesting theory.

"Take the next exit," Charles added. "The hospital should be to the right."

After following the signs for the emergency room, Victorine managed to find a parking spot safely away from all other cars. As they walked into the lobby, she escaped into the restroom to freshen up while Charles talked to the receptionist.

Victorine splashed some water on her face and when she looked up, she jumped at the sight of Daniel standing behind her.

"A road trip, huh?" He crossed his arms and leaned against the wall next to her. "Was that an attempt to get rid of me?"

Victorine let out a frustrated sigh. "I am not in the mood to argue," she grumbled, grabbing a paper towel and drying her face. "But if it makes you feel any better, I do intend to give her the most dignified death of them all."

"You're a monster." Victorine rolled her eyes and walked away from him. "Where are you going?"

"I need to pee." But just as she locked the stall, Daniel appeared in front of her in the cramped space. "Daniel!"

"How could you think that would make me feel better?"

Victorine pinned him to the stall with a glare. "You need to learn boundaries."

"And you need to thaw your heart—" Victorine covered Daniel's mouth as she heard someone walk into the restroom. "They can't hear me," Daniel spoke into her hand, his voice muffled, but Victorine shushed him anyway.

"Hi, honey. I'm okay." It was the voice of an older woman. Sounded like she was on the phone. "It was those old steps at the back of the house... No, you don't have to fix them... Fine, then I'll cook you dinner. Oh, I can still move just fine... yes, even for that position." She giggled like a teenager, and Daniel's eyes widened, making Victorine's cheeks burn. "Sorry, I can't do it tonight. I know... I'm gonna miss you, too."

The toilet flushed and Victorine noticed Daniel's foot on the lever. She glared at him while he flashed her an annoying smile. After smacking his head and pushing him behind her, she pulled the door open and walked out. The older woman stopped talking and Victorine felt her cheeks flush. Clearly that was a private conversation. She walked toward the sink, avoiding eye contact, and started to wash her hands.

"I'll talk to you later," the older woman said, hanging up the phone and taking the sink next to Victorine. She washed only one of her hands since the other one was wrapped in a cast, then she looked at Victorine's reflection in the mirror. "Just because I'm old doesn't mean I have to be boring, right?" Victorine wasn't sure how to respond to that, but then the older woman laughed. "I was talking about dancing, in case you were wondering."

"I wasn't thinking anything," Victorine hurried to say, rinsing the rest of the soap off her hands. After she dried them with a paper towel, she followed the older woman out, only to find Charles standing outside the door.

"There you are, Nonna," Charles said in greeting, and the older woman beamed.

"Charlie!" She wrapped him in a tight hug, pulling him down to her five-foot-two height. When he pulled back, he looked at Victorine.

"Nonna, this is Victorine, a friend of mine."

His grandmother turned around with the same beaming smile. "Oh, how pretty!" She was still addressing Charles. "It's about time you stopped pining for that witch and found yourself a nice girl."

"I was never pining," Charles grumbled as a nurse approached.

"Mrs. Wiseman, you really shouldn't be on your feet."

"I'm fine," his grandmother replied, brushing the nurse off. "I didn't fall because I'm old, honey. I fell because my patio steps were broken."

The nurse gave Charles a pleading look and he turned to his grandmother. "Stop giving them a hard time, Nonna. They want to keep you overnight for observation and I'm gonna need you to behave."

"Fine," she replied without any resistance, and the nurse gave Charles a baffled look. She had been giving them a hard time all day. "You both go ahead..." Nonna waved Charles and Victorine off

as she started back to her room. "Go enjoy your-
selves. Be loud. You have my blessing."

Be loud?

Victorine looked at Charles and, for the first
time, caught him blushing. "Sorry about that," he
said in a low tone, stopping short of his grandmother's room. "She can be a handful some-
times."

Victorine chuckled. "I can see that."

Charles shifted his weight from one foot to the
other. "Let me go say good night and let her know
I'll come back for her in the morning."

Victorine nodded, then let out a low grumble as
she realized she never got to pee.

As they pulled into the driveway, Charles
turned off the car and stared at his grandmother's house. Her Victorian-style porch wrapped
around the front with a gorgeous swing by the
window, but that wasn't what he was looking at.

"What's wrong?" Victorine asked, noticing the tension on his arm as he grabbed the steering wheel.

"I think I saw someone upstairs," he whispered, unbuckling his seatbelt.

"Okay?"

Charles glanced at Victorine with a concerned expression. "If anyone else was staying here, Nonna would've told me. And there's no other car parked nearby."

"Oh." Victorine suddenly mirrored his concern. "Do you think someone broke in?"

"Stay here." He jumped out of the car, and without thinking, she followed after him.

"Are you insane?" she whispered, following him around the back of the house. "We should call the cops."

"Grab your phone and get ready to dial," he whispered in reply as they reached the back porch. But instead of looking toward the house, he was staring at something in the yard.

"What?" Victorine asked, following his gaze.

"When did my grandmother get a hot tub?"

"Charles, focus."

"Right." He shook off the distraction then reached for a potted plant by the wooden steps.

When he lifted it, he seemed disappointed to find it empty.

"What's wrong?"

"Whoever's up there took the spare key." He tiptoed around Victorine and reached for a hidden baseball bat underneath the patio. "Stay behind me."

"Just so you know, this is exactly what happens before a character dies," she hissed, grabbing onto his polo shirt. "What if he has an ax?"

"I would be more concerned if he had a gun."

"Nonsense. A gun is too predictable."

Charles lowered the bat and looked at her. " Right...because that's exactly what he's worried about." She shrugged, and he shook his head. "Just take out your phone and get ready to dial 911."

"My phone's in the car," she whispered, and he shot her a look of disbelief.

"Why would you leave your phone in the car?"

"Where's yours?" she asked, and when he hesitated, she remembered he left it in the cupholder. "Exactly."

Charles reached for the door. It was unlocked. Victorine grabbed onto his shirt even tighter. "Maybe we should go back to the car?"

As they stepped inside, the wood floor creaked above them and Charles lifted the bat toward the stairs. As they tiptoed past the kitchen, Victorine grabbed a frying pan.

"Wouldn't a knife be better?" he whispered.

"Yeah, right. And see blood? Gross."

Charles opened his mouth to point out the irony of her being a thriller writer, but footsteps started descending the stairs. He pushed Victorine against the wall then hurried to the other side of the stairs. Victorine clutched the frying pan with shaking hands, but when the shadowed figure appeared next to her, she screamed. Jumping out from behind the railing, she swung the pan at the shadowed figure in front of her.

The man stumbled backward, dropping whatever was in his hand with a loud thud as she continued to scream. He crawled toward the door, but she hit him again, screaming even louder as she felt the impact against the metal in her hand.

When the light finally came on, Victorine spotted Charles on the floor with his hands protectively over his head. "It's me!" he yelled. "Victorine, you're hitting me!"

Victorine dropped the pan on the floor with her eyes wide. "Oh, my! I am so sorry!"

A piercing screech came from behind them, and Victorine turned around. A brown-haired woman was laughing so hard, she could hardly breathe. "Oh, Charlie. That was priceless!"

Charles huffed in frustration as he got back on his feet. "I'm glad you find it funny that we could've killed you."

She stared at him for a moment then doubled over laughing again. Victorine looked at Charles in confusion.

"This is my sister, Lindzee," he said, still rubbing his head.

"That. Was. Epic," Lindzee cheered, wiping the tears from her eyes. "Oh, how I needed this tonight. Thank you."

"Glad to be of service," he grumbled sarcastically. "What are you even doing here? Aren't you supposed to be on a trip with your boyfriend?"

"Yeah, well..." It wasn't until her laughter faded that Victorine noticed her eyes were red. It looked like she had been crying. "Alan and I got into a fight so... I canceled the trip and came to help Libby with her wedding this weekend. What are *you* doing here? And who's this?"

Victorine flashed her an embarrassed smile while reaching out her hand.

"This is Victorine, my neighbor."

"Neighbor, huh?" Lindzee smiled, taking Victorine's hand. "Is that what they're calling it these days?"

Victorine's cheeks flushed. "Oh, no. We're not—"

"Does Karen know?" Lindzee asked, giving her brother a look that Victorine couldn't quite decipher. "Because if she doesn't. She should."

"Did you know Nonna is in the hospital?" Charles said, changing the subject.

"What?" Lindzee gasped. "What happened?"

"She fell off the porch and broke her hand earlier today. That's why we came."

"Oh my goodness! I had no idea. I just got here like an hour ago. If I knew, I would've gone to see her."

"She should be released in the morning once the doctor makes his rounds."

"Have you told Dad?"

"I'm sure Nonna will call him when she gets home tomorrow."

"Charles—"

"Would you mind showing Victorine the room while I grab our stuff from the car? Thanks." He started toward the door without waiting for a response, and Lindzee turned to Victorine.

"Isn't he charming?" she teased, then led Victorine down the hall. "You should take the basement. It's not soundproofed, but it's a lot more private."

Victorine's cheeks burned like fire, and she wanted nothing more than to bury her head into the ground. "We're not together."

"Not yet." Lindzee glanced over her shoulder with a smirk. "But wait until you see how small the bed is."

Chapter 6

VICTORINE WOKE UP WITH a wave of laughter in the distance. With groggy eyes, she glanced at her watch. It was eight o'clock in the morning, and Charles was already up. He had slept on the carpeted floor, but his pillow was on top of the dresser.

After washing up and slipping into her jeans, she headed upstairs. In the kitchen, she spotted Charles' grandmother surrounded by other women her age. When Victorine approached, all the women turned to look.

"Oh, this is Victorine," Nonna introduced. "Charles' girlfriend."

Before Victorine could correct her, the women were already pulling her to sit by the island counter with them.

"How long have you two been together?" one of them asked, pouring Victorine a cup of coffee.

"Oh, we're not—"

"They want to keep it low-key," Nonna added with a wink, and Victorine wondered if it would make any difference at all if she kept correcting them.

"Charles has always been so private, hasn't he?" one of the women chimed in. "One minute we don't even know he's dating; the next he's engaged."

Okay! That was where she would draw the line. "We are definitely not engaged."

"Not yet, hon. But all the men named Charles in this family have married young," one of the women said, placing a piece of carrot cake next to the coffee cup. "And Charles the Third is no exception."

The Third? Victorine suppressed a laugh.

"That's right," another woman cut it. "And not only are they husband material, but fertile as a rabbit."

And I'm done here. Victorine stood with her coffee at hand. "I'm gonna finish this outside."

"Sure, hon." And just like that, they returned to their previous conversation like nothing had happened.

Victorine stepped outside and immediately regretted forgetting her jacket, but there was no way she was walking back through that kitchen.

"Have they named your babies yet?" Lindzee laughed from the rocking chair at the end of the porch. "Don't feel bad. A minute ago they were grilling me about babies, and I'm not even dating anymore."

"Anymore?" Victorine echoed, sitting next to Lindzee.

"Yeah, well." Lindzee shrugged. "That's life, right?"

Victorine wasn't sure what to say, primarily because she didn't know much about what a *love life* entailed. She had always broken up her relationships just in time to start a new book. Dating was a fun distraction, but that was all it was... a distraction.

"So, how long have you and my brother known each other?" Lindzee asked, looking across the patio. When Victorine followed her gaze, she spotted Charles on his knees, fixing the broken steps.

"We've lived in the same building for about five years now."

Lindzee nodded, still watching her brother. "He looks happy," she noted. "I haven't seen him smile like that in a long time." Victorine wasn't quite sure how to respond to that, so she didn't. "Alan and I were together for two years. It's hard to believe it's over."

"What happened?"

"He forgot our anniversary and left me waiting at the restaurant."

"Did you ask him why?"

"He says he can't tell me. I mean, I understand if he couldn't make it, but at least explain, right?" She looked at Victorine for reassurance. "Or am I being unreasonable?"

Victorine was by no means an expert—she could only go by relationships she had written about. "I would insist on a reason. He owes you that much."

Lindzee sighed. "Maybe it's for the best. There's so much happening at the hospital right now, I can't afford to be distracted by this. People are counting on me."

"Are you a surgeon, too?"

"I am."

"Do you like it?" Victorine asked, wondering if she, too, had been pressured by her father.

"I love helping people," she said with a genuine smile. "In fact, I'm working on coming up with a clinical trial, and now it's the perfect time because we just got some extra funding."

"Have you chosen anything?"

"Not yet, but I need to present something by the end of this week. Otherwise, they'll give it to someone else." She rubbed her tired eyes. "That's why this whole thing with Alan couldn't have happened at the worst possible time. My mind is so unfocused."

"Have you ever heard of Gama Astroplexia?" Victorine asked, and Lindzee gave her a curious look.

"Yeah, it's a rare blood disease."

"Well, in recent years the number of children being born with it is rising. And the only treatment they have is the same for leukemia, which I've been told is too aggressive for this disease."

Lindzee watched Victorine for a long moment. "I assume you speak from experience?"

Victorine nodded, then went on to tell Lindzee all about Ari's condition and her treatments. To Victorine's surprise, Lindzee asked to see Ari's medical file. Michelle would have to approve, of course, but Victorine would definitely make the call.

"Great!" Lindzee's eyes lit up with excitement. "I'm going to grab my laptop and start researching more about this right away. Who knows... maybe we could find a better treatment for her."

"That would be amazing."

Lindzee reached for Victorine's hand. "I will try my best." As she was about to stand, her eyes landed on her brother again, and she grunted. When Victorine followed her gaze, she spotted Charles still at the other end of the patio, but this time a blonde woman was next to him, holding a smoothie and giggling like a teenager.

"Who's that?" Victorine asked, scooting to the edge of her seat to get a better look.

"Karen." Lindzee spit out her name as if it left a bad taste in her mouth. "That woman almost ruined my brother. I was so glad when she broke off their engagement."

"Engagement?" That must've been what the women in the kitchen were talking about.

"He was head over heels for her," Lindzee said. "Then one day, she just broke things off."

Victorine felt a heavy tug inside her heart that she could only attribute to jealousy. "Why?"

Lindzee shrugged. "No one knows. But if I were you, I would go save him."

Though Victorine felt a tightness in her chest at seeing the woman touch Charles' shoulder, she reminded herself of a vital truth. "We're not together."

"Still..." Lindzee looked at Victorine. "If you care about him at all, you will want to keep that woman as far away from him as possible. Here..." She handed Victorine her bottle of water. "Go give him this and get him out of there."

Victorine grabbed the bottle and walked across the porch. When Charles saw her coming, he flashed her a smile that made her heartbeat quicken. "Thank you," he said as he took the bottle from her hand. "By the way, this is Karen."

Karen lowered her sunglasses only to have a better look at Victorine. "And I'm not sure he's told you, but we used to be engaged," Karen added smugly.

"He did, actually," Victorine replied, turning to Charles. "Now, would you mind taking a break and going for a walk with me?"

"Sure." He turned to Karen with a polite nod. "I'll see you around."

Karen forced a smile. which quickly vanished when her eyes met Victorine again. But Victorine couldn't care less. She looped her hand in Charles' arm then skipped up the newly renovated steps with him by her side.

"So..." He placed the water bottle on the wooden rail then wiped the moisture on his jeans. "Where to?"

"No idea," Victorine whispered, letting go of his arm. "I was just told to save you."

Charles laughed. "Is that how my sister put it?"

"Not just your sister." Victorine leaned against the rail, keeping her voice low. "Seems to me like everyone here thinks you need saving from that woman. Why is that?"

Charles let out a long breath as if bracing himself to revisit unwanted memories. "All right..." He tugged on her hand, which sent tingles up her arms. "Let's go take that walk."

"Wait, so she broke up with you because you quit medical school?" Victorine asked as they walked by the lake. "Why was that such a big deal to her?"

Charles shoved his hands into his pockets as he faced the water. "She never actually said it, but I'm pretty sure she was embarrassed."

"Embarrassed of what?"

He took a seat on a large rock and looked at Victorine. "Her father has his own practice downtown, and even before I went to college, everything was already set for me to work with him. He's been friends with my father for years. They went to medical school together. Anyway, when I quit my internship, he felt sort of betrayed—as did my father—and suddenly I became the disappointment of the family, both families. Then there was her mom, of course, filling her mind with garbage about how therapists don't make as much money as surgeons do and whatnot."

"That's terrible." Victorine sat next to him, shaking her head. "I am so sorry you went through that."

"It never bothered me," he said with a shrug, "but I guess I underestimated her need for approval."

When he said nothing else, Victorine nudged him with her shoulder. "Well, she didn't deserve you."

He smiled as he glanced at her. "Now you just sound like my sister."

"Do you still have feelings for her?"

"Not really," he said. "But I did spend a long time wanting her to say it."

"Say what?"

"The truth about why she wanted things to end," he confessed. "I have my assumptions, but... that's all they are—assumptions."

"Maybe she will now that she's jealous of you?"

He laughed. "She's not jealous of me. She's jealous of my attention shifting from her to you. In the end, it's still about her."

Victorine scrunched her nose. "That's really selfish."

"I don't think she realizes it, but I can read people pretty well. Why they behave a certain way. It's quite fascinating to me."

"Is that why you changed your career?" she asked, and he thought about it for a long time.

"It's not that I didn't like being a doctor," he confessed. "I guess, I just chose the mind over the body."

"And how exactly did that happen?"

He looked out to the water again. "During my second year in medical school, I got really over-whelmed and burnt out by all the pressure my father was putting on me. He had me working thirty hours straight. And pushing me to learn surgeries I wasn't ready for. I mean, the responsibility of having someone's life in your hands... it's already a lot of pressure."

"I can imagine."

"So, without anyone knowing, I went to see a therapist. I was only planning to go for a few sessions until I got back on my feet, but as time went on..." He paused, and she waited. "There was so much I didn't know about myself, and learning that was fascinating to me. It took almost a year for me to be able to separate the person I really was from the person everyone expected me to be. Especially my father. But when I finally set them apart..." He let out a breath. "I had never felt so free."

"What about your mother?" she asked, and he shook his head.

"As a biochemist, she wasn't thrilled either," he admitted. "But she never stopped talking to me for years like my father did."

"Wow... I am so sorry I kept the parking spot from you all these years."

Charles laughed, and she looked at him.

"I mean it!"

"I know you do. That's why it's funny." When their eyes met, something inside of her fluttered. She wanted to say something to encourage him, but her mind was too distracted by the stupid butterflies exploding in her stomach.

"I'm glad you're here," he whispered, and when his breath brushed her face, it smelled like peppermint.

"I'm sorry your family thinks I'm your girlfriend."

"I'm not," he said, cocking a brow.

She blushed. "Well, I guess it's good for them to see that you're not *pining* over your ex anymore," she added, wondering if that was one of the reasons he was thinking of. But he shook his head.

"I stopped *pining* for her after she slept with my best friend. After that, I just couldn't bring myself to fight for us anymore. Everything I felt for her was gone."

Victorine's eyes shot open as her brain went into overload. "Oh my flaming heck! That's it!" She jumped to her feet in excitement. "Charles, you're a genius!"

"I am?"

"Yes!" She grabbed his face in a rush of exhilaration and pressed her lips to his. But when he tensed, her brain glitched her back to reality and she froze. Ripping herself away from him, she pulled back with her eyes and mouth wide. "I. Am. So. Sorry."

He opened his mouth to speak, but she closed her eyes and moved away from him. *Crap on a stick! What was I thinking?* "I am so, *so* sorry. I just got super excited because I finally figured out how to get past the whole Emily-block-thing and... it was something you said, and I just... I didn't mean to..."

Charles raised a hand with a soft smile. "It's totally fine."

"Right." She wasn't sure why her heart felt suddenly tight, but she was too mortified to care. "I'm gonna go finish my book."

Charles nodded but didn't say anything else, and she walked away with her cheeks burning like fire. The taste of him still lingered on her lips, but she pushed the thought out of her mind, focusing on her book. On Emily.

And in that moment, Victorine braced herself to face the wrath of Daniel when he found out what she was about to write.

Chapter 7

VICTORINE TOOK A LONG hot shower in Lindzee's bathroom upstairs. For some reason the basement only had cold water. Maybe that would've been better considering the kind of thoughts she kept having about Charles after kissing him at the lake.

She still couldn't believe she had kissed him. The embarrassment twisted her stomach into a knot, but she still couldn't push the memory from her mind. Closing her eyes, she immersed herself under the hot water, letting out a long, relieved breath. At least she had been able to write over six thousand words that day. Emily was still alive, but not for long.

"Are you kidding me?" Daniel's voice startled Victorine, and she turned off the shower just as he pushed the curtain open. She fumbled with the towel as he stood there with a scowl. "That is garbage, and you know it!"

"I know you're mad," she said in a gentle tone, but it did little to soften his steel-like expression. "But I needed to weaken her will to fight, and the only way to do that was weakening her love for you."

"So you had someone tell her I *slept with her best friend*?" he yelled. "That never happened!" When he took another step forward, Victorine rushed out of the bathroom. "This is my life you're messing with!"

"I know, and I'm sorry!" She turned around just short of the patio door only to find Daniel holding up a small blackboard in his hand. "What are you doing?"

"Tell her the truth," he demanded, touching his fingernails on the board. Victorine gasped as goosebumps trailed up her arms.

"Don't you dare."

"Then give us a happy ending."

"It's not that simple."

"Then you leave me no choice." Daniel lunged toward her, scraping his fingernails against the blackboard. She ran away from him, covering her ears, cringing at the sound. By the time the noise stopped, she was outside on the dark patio, pressed against the ornamental railing. When she turned around, Daniel appeared inches from her face, jolting her backward. She screamed as she lost her balance over the railing, falling into the bushes with a loud thud.

Ouch. She grunted from within the bushes, opening her eyes to a night sky full of stars. As her vision began to focus, she noticed something white hanging on the railing above her.

A towel?

When a gust of wind blew, making her shiver, her eyes widened in panic. *Her* towel!

She gasped, rolling out of the bushes despite the aches from the fall and tried covering herself with her small hands and thin arms. The backyard was empty but laughter came from inside the house. The women had moved to the living room with their glasses of wine, and Victorine scanned the area for a way back inside. She spotted a used towel by the poolside and without any hesitation, she darted toward it. Halfway across the lawn, she heard the back door open and Charles' voice in the distance. She quickly jumped into the hot tub and turned it on so it bubbled around her.

"Hey." *Please, don't come over. Please, don't come over.* "I thought you were in the room finishing your book?" he asked, walking toward her with a young couple next to him.

"I was," she replied, sinking down to her jaw as they approached. "In fact, I should go back. Would you mind passing me that towel?"

"Oh, you don't have to leave. Let us join you for a bit." When Charles pulled his shirt over his head, Victorine's heart almost jumped out of her throat. She looked away, forcing herself to push the image of Charles' chiseled muscles out of her mind. "This is Libby and Matt, by the way."

The couple waved, also stripping down to their bathing suits, and Victorine hugged her legs underwater, forcing herself not to panic.

Crap on a stick!

"They'll be getting married tomorrow," Charles added, throwing his shirt aside and jumping in next to her. "We all went to high school together, and Matt's been drooling over Libby since freshman year."

"*That* he has," Libby teased, poking Matt on his side. When he leaned in to give her a kiss, Charles glanced at Victorine. As if she didn't feel mortified enough, he just had to look at her with a gaze so soft it reminded her of their kiss earlier.

"Quit flirting and jump in already," Charles splashed them with water, and Victorine's stomach flipped.

"I really should get going," she mumbled. "Charles, *please* hand me that towel." She gave him a pleading look, but he seemed totally oblivious to her desperation.

"Are you trying to get away from me because of what happened earlier?" he whispered, and she seriously contemplated drowning herself.

"Charles, please." Her stomach was already tied in a million knots. "Just get me the towel. I am begging you."

He let out a disappointed sigh. "Fine."

She felt slightly relieved, but before he could move, the hot tub timer turned off and the bubbles disappeared.

Crap on a gigantic stick! Victorine curled into a ball, hoping it would make her feel less bare, but nope. And when she caught Libby's wide eyes staring at her, she sunk lower into the water.

"Matt, we should give them some privacy," Libby said, pulling her legs out of the water, and Victorine pressed her eyes shut. She could only hear Libby dragging her fiancé away.

When she opened her eyes again, Charles was staring at her with his eyes wide. "Are you...?"

"Please, just get me a towel," she whimpered.

He reached behind him quickly, and after grabbing his own towel, he handed it to her. She wasted no time in wrapping it around her thin body. She was so mortified, she could literally die of embarrassment.

"Victorine, I had no idea—"

"Don't mention it," she said, jumping out of the tub and rushing back into the house, dripping wet. She bolted across the living room so fast, the chatty women didn't even notice anything out of the ordinary. Or maybe it was the wine. Either way, she was glad to finally be back in the basement.

She leaned against the closed door with her stomach still in knots. How was she supposed to face him after that? She felt so mortified, she could puke. When her stomach churned again, she started toward the bathroom, not even caring that the water was going to be cold.

"Victorine?" Charles' voice came from the door as it opened slowly, and her stomach flipped again. "Can we talk?"

"I cannot look at you right now," she said, turning her back to him and reaching for her duffle bag.

"Victorine, please." He walked in and shut the door behind him. "I didn't mean to embarrass you—"

She grimaced at the memory. "You didn't do anything. Really."

"Yes, I did." He came to stand next to her, but she couldn't bring herself to look at him. "I didn't know you were there waiting for me."

"Wait, what?" She shot him a look, feeling even more mortified than before. "Charles, I was not—"

"Just let me get this out, okay?" He stepped in front of her and cupped her face. "I'm sorry I didn't kiss you back earlier, but it wasn't because I didn't want to." When his eyes dropped to her lips, her breath got caught in her throat. "You caught me off guard, and I'm sorry I didn't react fast enough. But the truth is... I've been thinking about that kiss all day."

The world's biggest butterfly explosion fluttered in her stomach, sending chills all over her body. "You have?" she whispered, and he leaned in, his lips inches from hers.

"More than you know." When he brushed his thumb over her lips, all of her blood traveled south. "I would really like to try again... if I may?" His voice was soft and sweet and drenched in need—then his lips were on hers, and she gasped.

His mouth was hot and moist, and when she parted her lips, he deepened the kiss. She moaned against his tongue, and he pulled her closer, removing all space between them. He buried his hand in her hair, tugging it just enough to kiss down her neck. Shivers traveled down her body, and she pulled him with her onto the bed. Somewhere in her haze of pleasure, she felt his strong hand move up her bare thigh, and she ran her fingers through his buzzed hair. He let out a low groan filled with desire, and it was hands down the sexiest sound she'd ever heard in her life. But then he pulled back, panting.

"Maybe we should slow down," he whispered.

"Why?" she breathed, still clutching his hair.

"Because..." He sucke in a breath, and she opened her eyes. "I don't want this to just be a road trip fling."

"What are you saying?" she asked, trying to stop her head from spinning.

"I would like to at least take you on a proper date," he said, pushing a strand of hair from her face. "Then see where it goes."

"I don't think that's a good idea." She put her hands on his chest, and he rolled off of her.

"What's wrong?" he asked, watching her stand and walk across the room.

"I don't want to ruin what we have," she confessed.

"How is this ruining anything?" he asked, scooting to the edge of the bed.

"Because it's what I do," she said, turning to him. "Even if we have a wonderful time right now, eventually I'm going to ruin everything because none of my relationships ever last. I only ever dated men in between projects, and if I'm being completely honest, most of them were just for research."

"Maybe you haven't found the right person—"

"No." She frowned. "It's because my books are my priority. They have always been, and they always will be. And I can't ask someone to accept that. It isn't fair to them."

Charles stood and crossed the room until he was standing in front of her. When she looked up to meet his deep blue eyes, he smiled. "I'm not asking you to marry me, Victorine."

"I know that."

"Then stop worrying about what might *eventually* happen in the future. We're not there yet." He cradled her cheeks and pulled her toward him again. "We just had our first real kiss a few seconds ago. I don't expect you to suddenly put me above everything in your life. That wouldn't even be reasonable." When he flashed her another smile, she felt suddenly hot, and dropping the towel was under serious consideration. "Why don't we just focus on one day at a time? Be my date for the wedding tomorrow, and we can reevaluate things at the end of the night?"

Victorine leaned into his bare chest, and he wrapped his strong arms around her. "One day at a time," she whispered.

He kissed the top of her head. "One day at a time."

Chapter 8

IT HAD TAKEN ALL day to decorate the backyard for Libby's wedding. The sun had started its descent in the sky when the groom took his position next to Charles by a makeshift gazebo. Victorine sat next to Nonna and her date, but her eyes stayed glued to Charles. Those blue eyes could be seen from a mile away, and when he winked at her, she felt flutters all over her body.

The feeling scared her more than anything. She had never felt this way about anyone before, and though it felt exhilarating, it also made her feel like she was standing on the edge of a cliff.

"I know that look," Nonna whispered, snapping Victorine from her thoughts.

"Excuse me?"

"The way he's looking at you," she said, shifting her attention to her grandson and Victorine followed her gaze. "That's the same way *my* Charles used to look at me."

Victorine sucked in a breath, hoping the tightness in her chest was from the navy cocktail dress she'd borrowed from Lindzee, and not from the way Charles was looking at her. He finally broke his gaze when the bride appeared and started walking down the aisle, but it did little to help Victorine breathe again.

After the vows, the couple kissed and applause erupted in the backyard. The setting sun bathed the sky a dark orange, and the groom took the bride by her hand. They disappeared into the woods with the photographer to take their wedding photos. In the meantime, the town's women began to bring out the food and drinks while everyone sat at their designated tables.

"You look stunning," Charles whispered as he touched the small of Victorine's back. His touch sent electricity up her spine, and she shivered.

"Well, you don't look so bad yourself." she replied, blushing. "Though, I didn't peg you for a bowtie kind of guy."

He smiled. "Whatever the bride wants." He led her to one of the tables, and they took a seat across from his grandmother.

"How did you two meet, anyway?" Nonna asked as soon as they sat down. "Tell us everything."

"Well…" Charles glanced at Victorine, wondering how she would've liked to answer that question, but when she didn't offer him any help, he looked around the table. "We live in the same building, and one night she almost got electrocuted trying to play electrician."

Victorine looked at him, interested in why he picked that moment out of all other brief encounters they'd had before that. "Hey, I got the power back on, didn't I?" She nudged him playfully, and he grabbed her hand. When he didn't let go, she was surprised by how naturally they fit together.

"What about your parents?" Nonna asked. "Are they in New York, too?"

"No," Victorine replied, looking away from Charles. "But my sisters are. And it's been nice living close to them again."

"How many sisters do you have?"

"Four."

"No boys, huh?" Nonna's date chimed in. "I feel bad for your old man."

Victorine's father didn't live long enough to be an old man. Neither did her mother. They died in a plane crash when she was only five, but she wasn't about to share that with a bunch of people she didn't know.

"Oh my Word, you're not gonna believe this!" Lindzee came from behind them and crouched between Victorine and Charles with the widest grin. "I just got off the phone with Mark. They accepted my pitch for the clinical trial. Now they want to hear the whole presentation!"

"What clinical trial?" Charles asked.

"The one Victorine suggested; to find a better treatment, or even a cure, for Gama Astroplexia," Lindzee replied with a squeal. "I can't believe this is really happening!"

"Congratulations," Victorine said, but Lindzee shook her head and grabbed Victorine's hand.

"Thank *you* for the idea. My interns have already been gathering information on everything they can get their hands on. I will let you know what happens. And if it's approved, who knows..." She pulled back with a pleased smile. "Maybe you can come shadow me for a few days. Perhaps some research for your next book?" Lindzee winked as she stood, and Victorine smiled.

Once Lindzee walked away, Charles stood. "Would you come dance with me?" he asked, offering Victorine a hand.

They hadn't even had dinner yet, but... "Okay."

As he led her to the center of the dance floor, a slow song started to play, and he pulled her close. Though her body molded perfectly to his, something was off. He was holding her hand in a firm grip.

"Is everything okay?" she whispered, pulling back just enough to see his face. His jaw was tight.

"Why are you filling my sister's head with things you know nothing about?" His voice was sharp, and Victorine pulled back even more.

"Excuse me?"

"Gama Astroplexia?" Charles replied. "Do you have any idea how complex that blood disease is? And I don't mean whatever you read on Google." Victorine felt a stab in her chest as his expression turned even more serious. "Writing books about stuff like that must be really fun for you, but treating kids with that disease is not fiction. So, if you want to use me for your research, go ahead, but my sister is off-limits."

Victorine swallowed the knot in her throat and stepped back. "I'm sorry I got entangled with your family. It won't happen again." She walked away with her chest so tight, she could hardly breathe. But maybe it was for the best.

After all, ending sooner rather than later was always for the best.

The moon was bright in the night sky, bathing the dark lake in a silvery glow.

"Are you serious?" Michelle asked over the phone, and Victorine smiled as her bare feet dangled over the edge of the pier. It wasn't often that Michelle got good news—especially regarding Ari's treatments—so it felt good to tell her about the clinical trial.

"Nothing has been approved yet, but she would like to take a look at Ari's file. All of her tests and treatments and medications since she was born."

"Sure, I'll get on that right away," Michelle said, her spirits slightly lifted. "Thank you so much,

Vicky. The universe has really been looking out for her. I heard today that someone has been anonymously paying for her stay here at the clinic."

Victorine thought about telling Michelle that she was the one who had been paying for those bills, but she was worried Michelle would want to either pay her back or stop her from helping. "Ari deserves that and more," Victorine said simply.

"Yes, she does."

"Is she awake?" Victorine asked.

"No. Today wasn't a good day for her. But at least she'll get to go home tomorrow until the next set of treatments."

"She's gonna be fine, you know. We're all looking out for her."

"I don't know what I would do without you girls."

Victorine smiled. She felt the exact same way. "I'll come by as soon as I get back in town. Tell her I say hello."

"Sounds good. I'll see you then."

"Good night."

After Victorine hung up the phone, she stared at the reflection of the moon mirroring on the lake. But then she noticed the shadow of a man coming up behind her and screamed, staggering to her feet.

"It's me!" Charles threw his hands up, dropping his jacket, and she grabbed his arm as she lost her balance on the edge of the pier. She fell back, pulling him with her, and they both hit the murky water with a loud splash.

"What's wrong with you?" she snapped, swimming toward the shallow. "You can't sneak up on me like that!"

"I didn't know you startled so easily," he replied, and she turned around with an *are-you-kidding-me* expression.

"I write *thrillers*, Charles!"

"Then shouldn't you know better than to sit alone in the dark in the woods?"

She let out a frustrated grunt as she found her footing. When she stood, the icy November chill engulfed her wet body, making her shiver.

"I came to apologize," Charles said, pushing himself to his feet. "I shouldn't have said any of that."

"It's fine." She tried to pull away, but he touched her arm, and she stopped.

"My sister told me about your niece," he said, drawing closer to her. "I feel like a jerk."

"Yeah, well, you live and you learn." She tried to pull away again, but he stepped in front of her.

"I was just worried about my sister," he said. "A few years ago, she came to me about having suicidal thoughts. She never acted on them, and she's gotten a lot better since then, but getting involved with a clinical trial with sick kids... I was just afraid it would be too much for her."

Victorine met his eyes. "I had no idea."

"I know." He brushed his thumb over her cheek. "I should've talked about it with you instead of jumping to conclusions. I'm sorry. And about the things I said—"

"It's fine, really."

"No, it's not." He cupped her face. "When you walked away from me earlier, my chest felt so tight, it was hard to breathe."

She touched the back of his hand, holding his gaze. "That's exactly why we should end things here."

"I'm not afraid of getting hurt."

"But I am." She removed his touch from her skin and stepped back. "In fact, I'm terrified. Last time I got my heart broken, I couldn't write for a whole year. I tried but couldn't even come up with one coherent sentence. It was terrifying. I didn't think I would ever be able to write again. And I didn't feel for him half of what I've already been feeling for you—"

Charles' lips were on hers before she could take another breath. As he deepened the kiss, his tongue was as hot as his wet clothes were cold against her skin. His hands were strong as they moved down her back, lifting her up so she could wrap her legs around him. She needed to stop this glorious, all-consuming madness, but then her back was against the wooden beam with his body pressed against hers, and all of her senses were set ablaze. She moaned into his lips, and he let out a low grunt so sexy, she just about came undone.

She tore her mouth from his, gripping her unzipped dress. "Charles." The desire in his dark eyes stole what was left of her breath. "Yeah?" Flipping heck, she loved hearing him breathless. Loved it as much as she loved the hard press of his muscles all along her body as he held her so tightly that it felt like he would never let her go.

We need to stop, she wanted to say. But instead, she spoke the next thought that came to her mind. "I've never felt this with anyone."

He sucked in a breath as he met her eyes. "I will never hurt you," he whispered. "You have my word."

They laid on the grass under a blanket of stars, and when she snuggled deeper into his arms, he threw his jacket over her then kissed the top of her head.

"Ready to go back to the house?" he asked.

"Absolutely not. I already told you, not until everyone is gone." He laughed, and she slapped him flirtingly. "It's not funny! Libby already caught me flashing in the hot tub. I don't need everyone else seeing my broken zipper and jumping to conclusions."

"It got caught on the wood."

"Yeah, like they'll believe that. You, mister..." She poked him on his chest. "Are ruining my reputation."

"Am I?" He rolled on top of her, and she suddenly forgot what she was saying. "We could just spend the night here, you know?"

"Now, that's tempting." She kissed him softly, then felt his hand move up her thigh. She slapped it playfully, and he pulled back with a smirk.

"I'm trying to seduce you," he teased.

"Not in this filthy grass, you won't."

He laughed, rolling to his back and pulling her into his arms again. "Fine, then tell me more about you."

She laid her head back on his chest. "What do you wanna know?"

"At dinner, you avoided talking about your parents. Why is that?"

She felt a numbness in her heart at the thought of her parents. "There's not much to say. They died when I was five, and I went into the foster system. Changed homes every year—except for when I found my sisters. We stayed in the same home for two years together. But then everything changed again and we had to go our separate ways." Her heart ached a bit with *that* memory. "It was soon after that I started writing."

"Did you miss it?" he asked. "The homes you left behind, I mean?"

"Not really," she confessed. "I mean, even if I did miss some of them, I've always been pretty good at detaching myself from things I left behind."

"And how did you manage that?" he asked.

"I would just make myself believe I didn't want it anyway," she explained. "If I could kill those feelings, then I wouldn't miss it. And it wouldn't hurt anymore."

"But you didn't do that with your sisters?"

"Oh, I tried..." she confessed. "But it hurt more to forget them then it did to miss them."

"That's interesting," he murmured, and she lifted her head to meet his eyes.

"What is?"

"The timing of when you started writing," he said. "It may explain why you kill your characters."

She narrowed her eyes. "What do you mean?"

"Well..." He shrugged. "It would just be a theory, of course."

"Tell me."

He adjusted his position then looked up at the stars again. "It seems that growing up, you had to leave many lives behind. And it was painful, so the only way to move forward was to stop the pain. But the only way to stop the pain was to kill it—every thought, every feeling connected to your old life. Get rid of all of it. Then, and only then, would you allow yourself to move forward."

"So, what does that have to do with my sisters?" she asked, and he brushed her cheek with his finger.

"It could be that you projected that pattern onto your books because although you didn't want to get rid of your sisters, you still needed to get rid of something in order to keep moving forward."

"My characters..." Victorine mumbled in disbelief. "You really think so?"

"Like I said, it's just a theory."

"What about Emily, though?" she asked, intrigued. "Do you have a theory on that?"

"All I can think of is that you *want* to give Emily a happy ending, you just don't know how."

She gave him a puzzled look. "How to write a happy ending?"

"How to move forward from it."

Victorine sat up at the sudden realization and looked toward the lake. "So... I've killed my characters because I needed a sense of finality in order to move on?" When Charles didn't respond, she let out a chuckle. "And here I thought I just liked thrillers."

"Hey..." He sat up and brushed her cheek. "That was just a theory."

"But a very good one," she said, meeting his eyes. "And the more I think about it, the more it makes sense."

"They're fictional characters, Victorine."

"But look at what it says about me." She thought about Daniel, and how strong his love for Emily was. "I kept my characters from their happy endings because *I* didn't want them to go on living without me. How selfish is that?"

"We all have different ways of coping," he whispered. "You used your books as a means of escape to cope with your feelings—your emptiness. There's nothing wrong with that."

"Charles, I've been using my books as a crutch *not* to deal with my feelings..." She stood, and when an icy chill blew between them, she wiggled into his jacket. Moving to the edge of the water, she stared at the silvery lake for a long time. When she felt Charles behind her, she leaned back into his chest. "I've been hiding behind my books like a coward."

"You're not a coward," he said, nuzzling the top of her head. "You were just never taught to deal with your feelings. That's more common than you think."

When she shook her head, he turned her around and framed her face with his hands. "You've lost more in your life than most people have in a lifetime. And yet, here you are. Still standing strong." He peered into her eyes, and her heart beckoned for him. "That's not something to be ashamed of. It's something to fall in love with."

Her heart jolted as her mind echoed the word "love" over and over again.

"Sorry." He pulled back with a nervous chuckle. "I didn't mean to freak you out—"

She threw her arms around his neck and pressed her lips to his with such a strong desire, she couldn't even think straight. And when he squeezed her tight, she felt his strength in her soul. She parted her lips, inviting him to deepen the kiss, and when he did, she wanted nothing more than to feel his strength everywhere else.

Chapter 9

THE NEXT MORNING, VICTORINE woke up in bed with her head resting on a strong chest. She smiled as memories of the night before at the lake flooded her mind, causing an explosion of fireworks in her stomach. Though they only cuddled through the night, it still made her feel light and carefree as never before, and she lifted her head, eager to melt in his deep blues. But she spotted a pair of green eyes staring back at her instead.

Daniel!

She jolted back and fell off the bed.

"Good morning, love," he greeted in a teasing tone, rolling on his side to face her. "Quite a breakthrough last night, huh?"

She rose to her knees with a grumble. "I should've written you with a bell."

"Woulda, coulda, shoulda. Let's just get right to business, shall we?" He held up an envelope. "What is this?"

"Where did you get that?"

When she tried reaching for it, he pulled it away. "To all characters I've killed before," he read aloud. "What's this all about?"

"Charles suggested it." She finally snatched it from his hand then crawled back into bed. "But it's not for you, so don't worry about it."

"What are you hoping to accomplish with that?"

Victorine looked at the letter in her hand. "Closure, I guess."

"Is Emily in that letter?"

"No, she's not." Victorine turned to look at him. "What are you, anyway? A figment of my imagination? A representation of my subconscious?"

He shrugged. "I'm just a guy trying to save his girl."

Victorine sighed. "It's not that easy, Daniel. I don't know how to write a happy ending. How to do justice to your love for her. It's too strong."

"Why is that a problem?"

"Because I don't know what that feels like," she confessed, staring at the ceiling. "The only time I ever fell in love, my heart was shattered. Now, that's the only feeling I remember."

"What about Charles?" Daniel asked. "Can't you use him to suck up some inspiration?"

She looked at Daniel again. "Once I tap into that source, there's no going back."

"It doesn't matter because once you experience love without reservations..." He smiled. "You won't *want* to go back."

Victorine considered that for a moment. "You think so?"

"Trust me."

Victorine could feel what was left of her defenses crumbling. And though it scared her, she trusted Charles. "How did you turn out such a hopeless romantic?"

Daniel chuckled. "You have it in you, Victorine. You just gotta give someone the key."

She nodded then jumped up out of bed with a grin so wide, she didn't even feel like herself. "Okay. I can do this."

Daniel laid back with a pleased smile, throwing his hands behind his head. "Go write what's in your heart."

Other than someone walking upstairs, the house was pretty quiet. Victorine walked across the kitchen, thankful that Nonna and her friends weren't there to suck her into another conversation about babies. She was terrified enough about opening herself up for love; thinking about *Charles the fourth* would probably get her hyperventilating for the rest of the day.

She finally found Charles on the patio, sitting in the rocking chair next to his sister. Victorine stopped in the doorway and took a deep breath. That was it. No going back.

"I thought that's what you wanted?" Lindzee asked, and Victorine stopped.

"I thought so too, but..." Charles ran a hand over his buzzed hair. "After she opened up last night... I didn't feel anything."

Victorine stepped back into the house and pressed her back against the wall.

"Did you tell her that?"

"How could I? She's like a rollercoaster off the tracks, Zee."

Tears filled Victorine's eyes within seconds and she covered her mouth, muffling the sound of her cry.

"Why didn't you just get it over with last night?"

"I didn't want to hurt her feelings."

"I know, but... the sooner she knows your heart belongs to someone else, the better."

"I know."

Victorine rushed back to the basement and as soon as the door shut behind her, she dropped to the floor, giving in to her sobs. Her heart felt so tight, she could hardly breathe. But then she spotted her notebook on the nightstand, and her eyes went dark. She wiped the tears off her face and sucked in a breath. Though her heart was still aching, her mind had never been so clear. And in that moment, as she stared at what was left of her book, she remembered Daniel's last words...

Go write what's in your heart.

Charles walked in holding two cups of coffee just as Victorine zipped up her duffle bag.

"Going somewhere?" he asked with a soft smile as he closed the door behind him.

"Home," she replied in a cold tone, and he cocked his head.

"I thought we were gonna meet up with your sister?"

"Something happened at the writing retreat and she left. So, I'm going back home."

"All right, I'll start packing—"

"No need," she said, grabbing her jacket and slipping it on. "I already called a cab to take me to the bus station."

"Bus station?" When she didn't respond, he placed the coffee cups on top of the dresser and moved toward her. "Okay, what's going on?"

"I finished my book," she said, straightening her posture like a shield. "And that's what this road trip was all about for me, Charles. Nothing else."

He looked at her as if he didn't recognize the woman standing in front of him. "What's gotten into you?"

"You said to take one day at a time then reevaluate, right? Well, this is me reevaluating." She reached for the duffle back, but Charles pinned it to the bed.

"Is this what you really want?"

She pulled back so he couldn't touch her. "What I wanted was to finish my book. That's all that matters to me. That's all that will *ever* matter to me."

"What about all the things we said last night?"

"That was just for inspiration. Now, if you'll excuse me..." She yanked her bag away from him. "I have a book to publish."

Chapter 10

A FEW DAYS LATER, Anne-Marie still hadn't shown up to work. Victorine tried calling, but it was going straight to voicemail. She went to knock on Tess's office then waited for her to finish with a call.

"Please, tell me you have a bestseller ready for us?" Tess asked, stress clearly visible in the dark circles under her eyes.

Victorine lifted the completed manuscript without much enthusiasm. "Have you seen my sister?"

"She's on her way, and I suggest you say your goodbyes because I will kill her," Tess said, leaning back and rubbing her belly. "I am one week away from maternity leave, which is the equivalent to a fire-spitting dragon, and your sister is driving me nuts."

Victorine smiled despite her aching heart. "You're a good friend, Tess. I'm glad my sister's got you around."

Tess studied Victorine for a few seconds. "Are you doing okay?"

"Yeah." Victorine didn't want to talk about it. "Can you just make sure she gets this?"

"You're leaving it with me?" Tess's eyes widened in surprise. "Okay, you're definitely not well."

Victorine chuckled, placing the manuscript on Tess's desk. "Enjoy your time off. You deserve it."

As she walked away from the final draft of her book, her heart squeezed in her chest. There was no going back. She left the building and took a cab. Next thing she knew, she headed to the children's clinic.

As she walked into Ari's room, she spotted a nurse changing the bed sheets. "Where's Ari?" she asked.

"Upstairs for the last set of her treatments," the nurse replied. "Your sister's up there with her."

Victorine sighed as she sat on the recliner in the corner. "Would it be okay if I wait for them here?"

"Sure." The nurse finished making the bed then headed toward the door. "She'll be happy to see you."

Victorine forced a smile. "It's always mutual."

As soon as the nurse walked out, Daniel appeared by the window. He had his back to Victorine and her heart ached in her chest. Even if she apologized, it wasn't going to be enough. Nothing was ever going to be enough. There was no forgiveness for what she had done. What she had written.

"Very clever finishing your book on a cliffhanger." When he turned around, his eyes were gray and void of all emotion as if he'd been stripped of his soul. "I just can't believe you made *me* the killer."

A sickening feeling rose in her stomach. "You asked me not to kill her."

"Yet, you managed to give us a fate worse than death," he replied, his voice deflated. "Congratulations on your precious award. I really hope you get it."

"Why?"

"Because you'll see that it won't fill the void in your heart. Nothing will. Ever." When she didn't respond, he stood up straight and shoved his hands in his pocket. "Goodbye, Victorine."

"Daniel..." But before she could say anything else, he was gone. Still, she whispered to the empty room, "I really am sorry."

As Victorine got out of the elevator and walked down the hall, she spotted Lindzee coming out of Charles' apartment.

"Hey," Lindzee greeted, locking the door and turning toward Victorine. "I got your niece's paperwork, by the way. I was just about to call your sister. Michelle, is it?"

"Yeah, I just came from seeing her," Victorine said. "She has a lot of questions."

"I hope I'll have answers. I'm really nervous about the clinical trial presentation."

"You'll do fine." Victorine offered her an encouraging smile. "I'm sure of it."

"Maybe you could come over tonight for a glass of wine?" Lindzee asked. "I could use the company."

Victorine felt a stab in her chest at the thought of being in the same room with Charles. "I don't think that's a good idea."

"Oh, don't worry, my brother won't be home," Lindzee said. "In fact, I'll be moving in. I'm kinda hiding from my ex, and it's closer to the hospital. So...win-win."

"What about your brother?" She shouldn't care, but she couldn't help it.

"Depending on how the interview goes," Lindzee replied. "He might be moving to England."

"England?" Victorine swallowed the lump in her throat. "I thought he didn't want to take that job?"

"He didn't, but..." She shrugged. "When things didn't work out with you, he changed his mind."

"Then I guess it's for the best."

Lindzee frowned as if she had been expecting a different response. "I guess so."

"Well, I better get going." Victorine motioned toward her apartment. "I see you around, neighbor."

Lindzee's phone rang and she ignored the call. "I really hope you change your mind about coming tonight. Otherwise, I just might get desperate and give in to this *rollercoaster-off-the-tracks* woman."

Victorine froze with her key still in the lock. "What did you just say?" Victorine turned to face Lindzee again.

"Oh, it's nothing." She waved it off. "That's just what my brother calls Karen. And she hasn't stopped calling me ever since he told her they were never getting back together."

"But I thought he wanted to work things out with her?"

"He spent a long time considering whether or not he should," Lindzee admitted. "And after your little spat on the dance floor—which was not subtle by the way—Karen was all over him. She even begged him to take her back, but he didn't because he was falling for you. He should've told her that, but—"

"He didn't want to hurt her feelings," Victorine cut in, and Lindzee looked at her in surprise.

"Exactly. Did he tell you?"

No. And she had heard it all wrong. "Where is he right now?" Victorine asked, and Lindzee glanced at her watch.

"At the airport. His flight leaves in two hours."

Victorine took off running down the hall then rushed down the stairs and through the lobby. She almost got run over trying to catch a cab, and after an eternity in traffic, she finally arrived at the airport. Before the taxi even came to a full stop, she threw the money with an extra tip on the driver's lap then jumped out of the vehicle.

By the time she reached the desk, her heart was beating out of her chest. "I need a ticket to England," she spoke out of breath. "The flight that's leaving in an hour. I need a ticket for that one."

"They'll be boarding in fifteen minutes," the woman replied. "I'm not sure we have any seats left—"

"Then I'll take anything." Victorine slapped her credit card on the counter. "Just give me a ticket. Any ticket."

The woman took the card and typed on the computer. "Oh, why didn't you just say you have a ticket for that flight?"

"I do?"

"Is your name Victorine Leesky?"

"Yes."

"Then here you are. I'll print your boarding pass right away."

Lindzee.

By the time Victorine was given her boarding pass, she sprinted toward the gate. Going through security was both a nightmare and a blur. She only got to put on one shoe before she was bolting again.

At the gate, she was completely and utterly out of breath as she looked around for Charles. The terminal was empty, and she turned to the man standing by the podium.

"Have you started boarding this flight already?" she asked, still out of breath.

"Yes, we have." He reached out his hand. "Your boarding pass, please?"

She handed him the ticket with her ID, but as the man took it, he gave her a quizzical look.

"What?"

"Why are you wearing only one shoe?" he asked, and she looked down.

"Oh..." She let out an embarrassed chuckle then shuffled through her purse until she found her other shoe. "Security makes me nervous," she mumbled, slipping it back on.

"All set. Have a good flight," the man said, handing her back the ticket and ID. She darted toward the plane, but as soon as she reached the passenger entry door, she froze. Her knees weakened and her heart began beating at her throat.

"Are you okay, miss?" the flight attendant asked, stepping forward with a polite smile.

"Yeah." Victorine sucked in a terrified breath as all color drained from her face. "Just a bit of a... aviophobia."

The attendant smiled as if it was completely normal. "Here, let me help you find your seat."

Victorine leaned against the door, feeling slightly nauseated. "I'm actually looking for someone."

"I would be glad to help once you're in your seat," the attendant said, and Victorine turned toward the coach section. The narrow aisle just about caused her heart to jump out of her throat. She didn't normally feel claustrophobic, but that tight space made her start sweating profusely. "Follow me." The attendant led the way, and Victorine pushed her wobbly legs forward, holding on to each seat she passed.

"Here you go," the attendant stepped aside and motioned toward a middle seat. Victorine wiped her damp forehead with the back of her hand while she waited for a young man to jump up and let her through.

Once she took a seat, she hurried to fasten her belt then looked up at the attendant. "Miss, please..." she begged. "His name is Charles Wiseman. I need to speak with him."

"I'll go check on that for you."

When the attendant walked away, Victorine grabbed onto the armrest so tightly, her knuckles started to turn white.

"First time flying?" the young man next to her asked, but all she could do was nod. "Yeah, my girlfriend gets like that too."

"My parents died in a plane crash," she vomited the words as a wave of panic washed over her. "I think I'm gonna be sick."

"Do you need a barf bag?"

"What I need is to find Charles Wiseman."

"And you're sure he's on this plane?"

Victorine's eyes widened in horror. What if he wasn't? What if he changed his mind about leaving? "Okay, this was really stupid." She unbuckled herself and climbed over the young man like a cat recoiling from water. "Wait, don't take off yet!" she yelled, hoping the pilot would somehow hear her. "I wanna get out!"

"Victorine?"

She froze mid aisle and turned around. "Charles?" Even though she came looking for him, she was still surprised. Either that, or she was trying really hard not to panic in front of him. "Is it always this hot in here?"

"What are you doing here?" he asked, and she let out a nervous breath.

"I'm here because..." Her knees were shaking so much. It was shifting her focus from all the words she'd practiced on the way over. "I couldn't let you leave without knowing how sorry I am for all the things I said."

"You were pretty clear—"

"I was hurt," she confessed. "But that's no excuse for having said all of those terrible things to you. I was a jerk and I doubted you, and I'm sorry."

"So..." Charles moved toward her. "You were going to fly all the way to England just to apologize?"

"If that's what it would take for you to believe me, then yes."

He narrowed his eyes. "And what did you plan to do when you got to England?"

"Probably look for a horse tranquilizer so I could fly back."

Charles laughed. "You didn't think any of this through, did you?"

"Not at all." She chuckled, her stomach still fluttering with nerves. "I just needed to get to you before you left. But not to keep you from going," she clarified. "If you want to take that job, I'm not going to stand in your way. So, I'm not asking you to stay. I just need you to know that even though watching you leave is breaking my heart, it's okay. Because the pain is there to remind me that what we had was real, and I don't ever want to forget that. I don't ever want to forget you. Falling in love with you was the most liberating experience that has ever happened to me, and I will never kill that... no matter how much it hurts."

Charles brushed her soft cheek with his finger then looked into her eyes. "Then come with me."

She gasped at his unexpected request, and when she opened her mouth to speak, no words came out. There was so much to consider, her mind was spinning. "Charles, I..." Could she really do it? Leave everything and everyone behind? Her sisters? Ari? "I really am in love with you." It didn't answer his question, but she needed him to know that.

"Victorine..." He cupped her face in his strong hands. "I'm not moving to England."

She shook her head as if she hadn't heard him correctly. "You're not?"

"No. I was invited by a friend to give a lecture at a university, but that's it. I'll just be gone a week."

"But your sister said..." She stopped then gritted her teeth. "She tricked me."

"Seems so," he said with a chuckle. "So, what do you say? Want to spend a week in England with me?"

She wrapped her arms around his neck, her nerves fading away like a thunder in the distance. "In that case, I would love to go to England with you."

He wrapped his arms around her thin body and lifted her up, nuzzling her neck. "I'm never going to let you go ever again."

"You won't have to," she whispered. "Because I'm never walking away from you again."

He pressed his lips to hers. It was warm and soft and gentle. But she still pulled back to look him in the eyes. "We are coming back, right?"

He chuckled, lowering her back to the ground. "Of course we are. Our lives are here. And, something else we can't forget..." He flashed her a heart-stopping smile. "I just got a new parking spot."

Epilogue

S EVERAL MONTHS LATER...

Daniel's eyes filled with tears as he watched Emily walk toward him down the aisle in the most beautiful white dress he'd ever seen. She looked like an angel sent just for him. Not only to guard his heart, but to save him from the claws of darkness. Though he'd been framed for murder a year ago, she never believed it—not for a second—and if it hadn't been for the light of her love to guide him back, he would have been lost forever.

'I love you,' she mouthed to him as he took her hand. His heart felt lighter than air as he reveled in her radiant smile. She was his savior in more ways than she would ever know.

'My love for you has no bounds,' he whispered, pulling her close. *'I will defy even the impossible if it means saving you.'*

And with those simple words, he pressed his lips to hers, vowing to love her forever.

Victorine closed the book with a pleased smile. The crowd of women in the library listening to her reading had tears in their eyes. Never did they expect Victorine Leesky to write a sequel, let alone one with a happy ending. It was the first book where she didn't kill her female character, but the readers seemed okay with that because it was also the last book in the series, and closing it with a happy ending after so much tragedy seemed only fitting.

After the book signing was over, Ari ran around the table and hugged Victorine. "I knew it!" she beamed, squeezing her aunt tightly. "I knew they would end up together!"

Victorine laughed. "Yes, they do. Despite all odds, their love prevailed." She looked up to find Michelle holding up her phone. "Are you filming?"

"Yeah, Judy and Faye couldn't make it, so they asked me to take a video," she replied, ending the recording. "So, a happy ending, huh? Who are you, and what have you done to my sister?"

"Uncle Charles!" Ari jumped down from Victorine's lap and ran to Charles' arms.

"Ah, there's the answer," Michelle teased, and Victorine stood to give her sister a hug.

"I'm glad you came."

"Oh, Ari's been looking forward to this since you told her about it," Michelle said. "So, where to from here? I heard you announce that you will be taking a break from thrillers for a while."

"Only for a little bit," Victorine confessed. "Since Anne-Marie branched out on her own, I thought I could help her out by writing some romantic suspense under a pen name. But we'll see how it goes."

"Speaking of Anne-Marie, where is she?"

"I saw her earlier," Victorine said, looking around. "Tess must've gotten her, I'm sure. But she'll be joining us for dinner, though. Will you?"

"Yeah, count us in. Today was a good day for Ari."

"Any word on the clinical trial?" Victorine asked.

"Yes, and no." Michelle looked over her shoulder to make sure Ari wasn't nearby, then lowered her voice. "I need to get my mother to sign the paperwork, and she's nowhere to be found. It's been a nightmare."

"Anything I can do?"

"Oh, you've done so much already." Michelle waved it off. "But let's not put a damper on the evening. I'm gonna look for Anne-Marie and we'll meet you at the restaurant."

Michelle called for Ari, and she ran back, giving Victorine another hug before walking away to look for Anne-Marie. Charles walked around the table and pulled Victorine close. "So, how does it feel?"

Victorine melted into his arms with a pleased smile. "Feels good. I mean, it'll take some getting used to, but I'm very happy with how the sequel turned out."

"I'm proud of you." He kissed the tip of her nose. "I'm also very much in love with you."

She smiled up at him before pressing her lips to his. "I'm very much in love with you too."

"Does that mean I get an autograph?" he asked, grabbing a copy of her book from the table and handing it to her.

"That depends," she teased. "Are you giving it to your secretary?"

He smiled. "Not this one."

"Okay then." She uncapped the marker then flipped the book open to the title page. When her eyes landed on a shiny circle taped to the center of the page, she gasped.

"What is this?" she asked, looking up to meet Charles' eyes.

"What does it look like?" He flashed her a heart-melting smile as he removed the ring from the tape and got down in one knee. "Victorine Leesky... will you marry me?"

Her mouth dropped open as Charles' deep blue eyes beckoned for an answer. "Yes!" She beamed. "A million times, yes!"

He pushed the ring onto her finger then jumped to his feet. She wrapped her arms around his neck as he lifted her off the ground and spun her around. An explosion of butterflies fluttered all over her body, and she giggled until her feet found the floor again. Only when she pulled back did she realize the amount of camera flashes in their direction.

Her sisters and Ari cheered a few feet away. Michelle was back to filming, and Anne-Marie was clapping next to Lindzee.

Victorine turned to Charles. "They knew?"

He nodded. "Ari was the true accomplice, though," he confessed, winking at her as she stood in front of Michelle with a wide grin. "She's the one who taped it to the book."

Victorine hung herself on his neck again, drowning in his charm. "This couldn't have been more perfect."

"I'm glad you think so." He gave her a tender kiss on the lips. "But I'm mostly glad to be the one to give you your happy ending."

"This is not a happy ending," she corrected. "This is only the beginning."

THE END

Excerpt
My Ex and His List of Demands

OLD FLAME. NEW SPARKS. And a second chance at love.

When it comes to light at Anne-Marie's publishing house that she once dated reclusive bestselling author Sean Weston in high school, she's given a choice: get her ex to sign with their publishing company or find a new job.

Sean's never forgotten the first girl to break his heart, so when Blazed Hearts Publishing makes him an offer, he requests Anne-Marie as his editor. But first she must spend a week with him on a writing retreat, and if she survives his list of demands, he'll sign the contract.

The chemistry between Sean and Anne-Marie is as potent as his juicing, and Anne-Marie hasn't hiked since she was a teen. Who knew a lit-

tle blackmail and some sizzling romantic inter-
ludes could make Anne-Marie reconsider her life's
choices?

Keep reading for an excerpt...

My Ex and His List of Demands

ANNE-MARIE HADN'T HEARD HER EX'S name in over two years—when his latest bestselling novel hit the theaters and was a blockbuster sensation. Or as she would put it, yet another slap in her face. But this morning, at Blazing Hearts Publishing, she couldn't ignore the buzz.

The third book in his series had just hit the shelves, and Anne-Marie's boss just happened to be his number one fan. Why anyone enjoyed alien science fiction was a mystery to Anne-Marie, but to each his own.

She retreated to her office, but it wasn't much of an escape. Either the walls were too thin or his name—Sean Weston—was echoing in her own mind.

Despite her best efforts to focus on the manuscript she was editing, his name kept bringing back a flood of unwelcomed memories. And the fact that the manuscript she was working on was a romance novel made it even harder to concentrate.

"You're needed in the conference room," Tess's voice came from the door.

Anne-Marie begrudgingly looked away from the computer screen. She had just started to get on a roll without thoughts of Sean interrupting her mind. "If this is about my sister's manuscript—"

"It's not about Victorine," Tess said quickly. "Now, hurry up."

Anne-Marie arched a brow. If she was being hurried by her bestie who was eight months pregnant, then it had to be important. But if the meeting wasn't about her sister's manuscript being late, Anne-Marie had no idea what it could possibly be about. They had already discussed pending assignments at the noon meeting. What could've changed in only a few hours?

As soon as Anne-Marie appeared at the door of the conference room, all heads turned in her direction. There were only five people sitting around the oval table, but she recognized one of them as being her boss's boss. It was a big deal—whatever the meeting was about.

"There you are." Astrid smiled as she usually did with her clients, but never with her employees.

Something was definitely up. "Please, come on in."

Anne-Marie stepped inside, her legs slightly wobbly. She didn't normally feel nervous about work meetings, but having all eyes on her made her uneasy. As if they knew something she didn't.

"You're gonna want to sit down for this," Tess whispered as she pulled up a chair beside her. Anne-Marie didn't argue. She took a seat next to Tess and looked nervously around the room.

"Would you like a soda?" Astrid asked with what almost looked like a cunning smile on her face. Astrid was a shark, so any friendly gesture could be seen as a prelude to getting bitten in the behind. Was Anne-Marie about to get fired? No. Her boss wouldn't be offering her a soda if she was about to give her the boot. Would she?

A hard kick came from Tess under the table, and Anne-Marie winced. "Soda sounds great. Thank you."

Astrid looked at her assistant, standing in the corner, as if waiting for her to move. Once the young woman realized she was supposed to be getting the soda from the mini fridge, she practically sprinted across the room.

"I was just telling Mr. Fanning what a wonderful addition you have been to our team," Astrid said with her best smile.

Definitely a stellar compliment, and very well merited since Anne-Marie put her heart and soul into every project, but Astrid wasn't the type. So, either she was showing off to her superiors or whatever blow was coming her way was about to cripple her.

"Thank you," Anne-Marie managed to reply, hoping no one noticed the shakiness in her voice. Tess gave her a supportive glance as if there was nothing to worry about, but somehow, Anne-Marie had a feeling that, in just a few seconds, that wasn't going to be true.

"As I was saying..." Astrid shifted her attention to Mr. Fanning, though still motioning toward Anne-Marie. "Anne-Marie is one of the brightest editors we have in-house, and she has an excellent eye for catching bestsellers. Because of her, we represent Victorine Leesky, and her thriller novels have given us quite the spike in the charts. And her latest release is only about a few weeks away."

Victorine was Anne-Marie's sister. She wondered why Astrid failed to mention that part—it was, after all, a huge reason why they got the contract with her in the first place. And why was she showering Anne-Marie with compliments? It wasn't that she didn't feel she deserved them. She sure did. She worked her butt off seven days a week for over five years with Blazing Publishing, but it wasn't like Astrid to be so vocal in her praise for no reason.

Anne-Marie's hands began to sweat as Astrid continued listing more of her accomplishments in the company. Being in the spotlight always made her slightly uncomfortable. She grabbed the soda that had been left on the table in front of her and popped it open. The soda exploded. Anne-Marie sealed it with her lips and frantically slurped it up to prevent it from spilling, but it dripped down her arms and onto the table. Her boss stopped talking as all eyes were once again on her. Anne-Marie's cheeks reddened, and she wryly lifted the half-empty can as a weak apology.

Tess wiped the sticky droplets from the glass table, then handed Anne-Marie a fresh tissue and sat back as if nothing happened.

"Anyway, long story short..." Astrid spoke with forced patience, and Anne-Marie took a thirsty gulp of the fizzling liquid. "Anne-Marie will help us sign with Sean Weston. Turns out, they were high school sweethearts."

Soda spewed out of Anne-Marie's nostrils. Tears stung her eyes as she gasped and choked on the fizzy liquid, her throat burning.

"Excuse me?" Anne-Marie asked in a nasal tone as everyone stared at her. "Did you say... Sean Weston?"

"Yes," Astrid said, though still talking to Mr. Fanning. "And we are pretty confident she will follow through. So, you have nothing to worry about. I will forward you the contract as soon as we get it."

The contract? Anne-Marie was going to faint. How in the world could Astrid make such promises? Especially when it came to her and Sean Weston.

"Very well, then." Mr. Fanning stood, as did everyone else. "We look forward to the good news."

"You'll have it by next week."

Next week? Anne-Marie knew that standing and walking them out was the proper thing to do, but she couldn't move. Her legs turned to mush, as did her brain. It wasn't even the sky-high expectation her boss had placed on her shoulders, but how in the world did she even find out about Anne-Marie's past with Sean? It had been almost ten years since they last saw each other. Since she broke his heart and walked away from whatever was left of their relationship.

"You and Sean Weston were high school sweethearts?" Tess's low voice snapped Anne-Marie back to the present. "And you didn't think to tell me?"

Once everyone was gone, Astrid leaned on the table next to Anne-Marie. "Not only that, but they were caught in his pickup truck."

"What?" Tess screeched.

Anne-Marie buried her face in her hands, feeling the heat in her palms as she sank in her seat. They were caught kissing, but somehow her boss made it sound so much worse. As had the cop that called her foster parents. Not only were the two love birds parked in a no trespassing area, but it was past Fern Oak's curfew. After almost ten years, one would think she would be less mortified, but it was just as embarrassing now as it had been then.

"It wasn't like that," Anne-Marie muttered, even though she knew it was useless. "It all started with a dare, then a prank, because Sean's brother just couldn't help himself—"

"Whatever the case," Astrid cut in. "You are going to meet with him and get him to sign a contract with us."

With one perfectly manicured fingernail, Astrid slipped a photograph from a folder and slid it across the table. Anne-Marie pulled the picture closer.

A girl smiled at her from the photo. She wore a denim jacket with jeans and boots. Her eyeliner made her brown eyes look darker, pink gloss coated her lips, and her brown hair was thrown wild with the wind.

Anne-Marie found herself smiling back at her younger self, remembering the carefree days.

Then she looked at the boy. He was leaning against the truck, his arms wrapped around young Anne-Marie's waist. Sean's hazel eyes were as green as the Jets jersey he wore, and his grin managed to be both innocent and naughty at the same time. And those irresistible dimples—she'd been a sucker for them. His light brown hair was hidden by a Jets cap, but she didn't need to see it to remember how the strands felt sliding through her fingers.

She tore her gaze away from the happy couple and looked up to Astrid. "I understand why you may think I'm the best person for this," she said, pushing the picture away. "But what you must know is that Sean wants nothing to do with me. In fact, I'm pretty sure that if he finds out I even work here, he will not sign with you. So, for the sake of your golden opportunity, I should just stay as far away from this as possible."

"I highly doubt that," Astrid replied.

"Oh, but it's true," Anne-Marie insisted. "I broke his heart and—"

"We already told him you would meet him."

Anne-Marie's next words got caught in her throat. "You did what?"

"He's at a writing retreat this week, and we booked you a room," Astrid explained. "He has agreed to hear your pitch so... make it a good one."

Seeing Sean again? Her stomach churned, and she was fairly certain she was going to puke. "I'm sorry, Astrid. I can't do it."

When Astrid smiled, Anne-Marie could see a hint of annoyance that wasn't there before. "I don't believe you're being given a choice here." She folded her arms across her chest. "You are going and that's final."

"And if I don't?" Anne-Marie's voice shook with nerves. She didn't mean to challenge her boss, but Sean had a way of getting her to lose all common sense and do reckless things. Hence, how she ended up fogging the windows of his truck.

"If you don't meet his demands," Astrid said firmly. "You can kiss your job goodbye."

"His demands?" Anne-Marie echoed.

"Yes. According to him, he has professional demands." Astrid added, "And as long as you meet those demands, he will consider signing with us."

Anne-Marie had officially lost her voice. No, lost her mind, because she knew that, no matter how much she dreaded this assignment, she was going to have to do it. She was going to have to get the contract or her career with Blazing Hearts was over and she would have to start fresh at the bottom of another publishing house. And since her career was pretty much the sum total of her life, it wasn't exactly a threat without teeth.

"He's not going to sign a contract because he and I had a fling in high school. It was fun, but it wasn't that serious."

Now she was flat-out lying. Sean Weston had meant the world to her from the moment they started dating. She would've married him if he had proposed, even in high school. He also had set the gold standard in Anne-Marie's kissing scale. Editing a kissing scene was her favorite part of the job, not only because she was a good editor, but because she knew exactly what a great kiss felt like.

Astrid laced her fingers together. "I tell you what. You do this for me, and I'll repay you."

There was no money on Earth that would ever be worth her groveling to her ex, but she loved her job, so she listened and tried hard not to pout.

"You get Sean Weston to sign the contract with us, and I will consider accepting sweet romance manuscripts and let you be in charge of the queries."

Anne-Marie's jaw just about dropped to the floor. That was all she'd wanted since she started working there five years ago. She'd been pitching the idea for three of those five years and had been shot down more times than she could recount. She knew asking a steamy romance publishing house to accept sweet romance books was a long shot, but she never gave up, and it was finally paying off.

Except, that also depended on Sean signing the contract.

"What's with the bitter face?" Astrid asked, cocking her head. "I thought you would be ecstatic with the offer?"

"Oh, I am," Anne-Marie replied. "I'm just... processing everything."

And trying to make sense of how on Earth advancing her career suddenly became about meeting her ex's demands. It had to be karma.

"Good. Then bring me a signed contract and the promotion is yours." Astrid reached into her purse and handed Anne-Marie an envelope. "Here's your plane ticket and hotel check in. Go make us proud."

"You did what?"

Sean stretched out on the lounge chair at a retreat overlooking the lake and tried not to laugh at the horrified tone in his sister's voice.

"As your agent, I must say that signing with Blazing Hearts is a huge mistake. They specialize in romance, Sean. You write about aliens. Should I keep going?"

"It's Anne-Marie."

A loaded pause. "Are you kidding me?"

"Liz—"

"She breaks your heart, flees to the big city, and now uses her history with you to advance her career? She's got some nerve."

"It wasn't her idea," Sean explained. "It was her boss, and I'm pretty sure she's dreading this meeting just as much as I am."

"Are you, though?"

He'd been asking himself the same question for days, and though deep down he knew the answer, he wasn't about to share the pathetic truth with his sister.

Liz let out a long breath, and if Sean had to guess, she was probably rubbing her face in frustration. "Are you sure you want to go down that road again?" She sounded concerned, and Sean couldn't blame her. Only his sister knew just how much Anne-Marie had broken him. She was the one who helped him pick up the pieces.

"There is no road," he assured her. "This is just business."

"Then why don't you just call her?"

After so many years, he didn't want to be reunited with Anne-Marie by telephone. He wanted to see her face at the same time he heard her voice. It was just curiosity—for old times' sake.

"I'm just saying..." Liz continued. "With a movie premiere coming up and a deadline approaching, are you sure you're in the right mind space for this?"

"Relax. I know what I'm doing," he said, stretching his legs and sipping on a green juice. The sound of birds chirping on the ferns above adding to his relaxed mood. "No need to panic."

"This better not be a prank. I've had enough of you and Craig over the years," Liz grumbled. Though Craig was their oldest brother, he acted like the youngest. Sean had spent years wondering if his brother would ever grow up.

"This is not a prank," Sean assured her. "I've grown out of that sibling competition indefinitely. Especially after the last one."

His sister was quiet for a long time. "Craig really did cross the line on that one."

"I don't want to talk about that."

The silence on the other end lasted so long Sean thought Liz might have hung up on him. But no such luck.

"Sean, speaking not only as your sister but as your agent, I think this is a terrible idea. Professionally and personally."

"Maybe..." He crossed his legs at the ankles as he watched the sunset over the lake. "But if I'm going to move on, I need to do this."

Heat traveled to her cheeks, and she thought about unbuttoning her blazer. Though, what she really wanted to do was ditch the jacket entirely and allow the cold breeze to cool her down.

Sean lifted a finger, and the waitress approached their table, order pad in hand. "What can I get for you?"

Anne-Marie watched in silent amusement while he ordered them both her personal favorite—fish and chips with extra fries.

When the waitress left, Anne-Marie gave him a scolding look. "That's more calories than I've consumed in the last two years, Sean."

He waved away her halfhearted objection. "Let's get down to business, shall we?"

He leaned back in his chair and crossed his arms. It was probably supposed to look intimidating, but all the gesture really did was draw attention to how tan and incredibly well defined his biceps were against his polo shirt. Typing definitely wasn't the only activity he did.

"My sister doesn't think Blazing Hearts is a good fit for me," he said.

Professionally speaking, Liz wasn't wrong. But Anne-Marie also knew that Liz Weston would rather swim in shark infested waters than see Anne-Marie near her brother again. Or better yet, feed Anne-Marie to the sharks.

"We are making an effort to branch out to genres other than romance," Anne-Marie assured him. "A bestselling sci-fi would make a great brand for the marketing expansion."

Sean narrowed his eyes, studying her. "So, you don't think my books qualify as romance?"

"Your books are science fiction."

"Because they have aliens?" When Anne-Marie didn't respond, he smiled. "You never read my books, have you?"

Anne-Marie fidgeted in her chair. "I can't say I have."

The corner of his lips lifted a little. "Then how about we start there?"

"Where, exactly?"

Sean dug into a crossover bag on the seat next to him and pulled out a paperback with a spaceship on the cover. He slid it across the table.

"What is this?" she asked.

He arched a brow. "You mean to tell me you don't even know what my covers look like?"

Of course she did, but that wasn't her question. "Why are you giving it to me?"

"How can you edit book four if you haven't even read book one?"

Tingles travelled down her spine, but this time, it was a lot more to do with panic than nostalgia. "I'm not sure what you've been told, but I won't be your editor."

"I've been told that I could choose any editor I want. And from what I hear, you're the best one there. I would be doing a disservice to my books if I didn't select the best, wouldn't you agree? Professionally speaking, that is."

Her mouth dropped open. "Sean, you cannot be serious."

"It's just business—"

"It's not just business." She placed a hand over the book. "This is the reason we broke up."

"Okay. There's no need to make this personal."

She threw her head back and laughed. "I'm making it personal?"

The waitress brought their food, buying Anne-Marie enough time to calm herself and not say something she would later regret.

Sean never had a mean streak—if there was no chance of him signing the contract, he wouldn't be asking her to read his book. The book that destroyed their relationship. He'd never had it in him to humiliate somebody for the sake of his own enjoyment.

That didn't mean he wasn't going to have her jumping through hoops, of course. Apparently, an entire flaming series of them.

"And if I say no?" Anne-Marie asked.

Sean shrugged as he ate some of the fries. "Then you can tell your boss there's no deal."

She shook her head. "You're unbelievable."

He flashed a cynical smile. "And you're just as beautiful as I remembered. Especially with a perpetual scowl, such as the one you have right now."

Though Sean had no poker face, she couldn't read him for the life of her. What did he really want from her? The instincts that had skyrocketed her to the top of her career were giving her nothing, except the feeling he was setting her up for something she might want no part of.

"So, once I read your book," she said finally. "Then what?"

"Books," he said, emphasizing the plural. "Books two and three should be in a flash drive in your room. You need to read those too."

She chewed her lip, biting back the words she really wanted to say. "And then?"

"Then we chat about them." He smiled. The dimples were about as pronounced as she'd ever seen them. "This is a writing retreat, and we'll be here for a week."

"Wait..." Her brows shot up. "You want me to stay here... with you... for a week?"

The length of time hardly mattered, since she couldn't return to New York without the contract anyway. But she would have liked more details. Would her boss pay for the whole week, or would she have to share a room with him at some point?

"You get through the three books and understand the essence of my characters," he said, "and you can take home a signed contract."

Three books. Three hundred thousand words before they could even talk about the contract.

Suddenly, looking for another job didn't seem so bad. Not if it meant she wouldn't have to work with him moving forward. Although, there was always a possibility that Astrid would do her a solid and assign another editor to work with Sean for the long haul.

"Anything else on your list of demands?" Anne-Marie asked sweetly. Though, what she really wanted was to wipe that beaming smile off his face.

"Oh, plenty. But how about we tackle one at a time, shall we? First..." He slid the book across the table and tapped the cover with his finger. "You get started on this and let me know when you finish."

Anne-Marie stifled a groan as she snatched the book. She pulled a manilla folder from her purse and tossed it on the table. "Meanwhile, you can hold onto that. The contract is inside."

He put it aside without so much as a glance. "I'll have it sent to my sister. Now…" He pointed to the fries. "Shall we finish what we started?"

Buy *My Ex and His List of Demands* on today!

Also By Jessie Cal

<u>Trouble in Love Series</u>
My Best Friend and My Odd Side Job
My Best Friend and the Honeymoon Game
To All Characters I've Killed Before
My Ex and his List of Demands
And more...

<u>Disarray Series</u>
Memories Lost
Memories Restored
Memories Recalled
Boxset
...also in audiobook

<u>Anomalous Series</u>
Anomalous Secret

Anomalous Rogues
Anomalous Rescue
and more...
...also in audiobook

<u>Fairytales Reimagined</u>
Queen of Snow
Red Arrows
Beastly Secrets
Pure as Snow
Above the Sea
and more...

Connect with Jessie

Sign up to her newsletter at jessiecalauthor.com

for weekly updates.

Follow her on Instagram

for daily laughs and teasers.

Follow her on BookBub

for new release alerts.

Follow her on Goodreads
to review her books

About the Author

USA Today Bestselling author Jessie Cal has written over eighteen romance and suspense novels. Her books are known for their drama, romance, twists and turns, and passion that gives you all the feels.

Jessie lives in a small southern town with her hubby. When she's not visiting family, getting together with friends, or cuddling with a book, she's writing her next novel.